D1234199

POISON
IS THE NEW
BLACK

WITH BONUS STORY:
TASTE OF CHRISTMAS

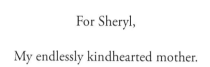

For Sheryl,

My endlessly kindhearted mother.

TASTE OF CHRISTMAS

POISON IS THE NEW BLACK
STARTS PAGE 43

1

I WAITED ON THE COLD park bench, borrowed ice skates in my lap, and hugged myself for warmth. I'd dressed for exercise rather than spectating.

Families and couples glided around on the artificial icy expanse in front of me, laughing and screeching from near collisions. A smile played on my lips. It was a beautiful winter Christmas Eve in Los Angeles, and I had a date.

My first in two years. With a man who was drool-worthy enough to have overtaken my daydreams months before I'd allowed myself to feel anything for him, and more importantly, with a man whom I could rely on. Someone who'd always have my back, as long as I wanted him there. Maybe even when I didn't.

I'd only been ice-skating once before. Unsurprisingly, it wasn't a common pastime in the sweltering heat of South Australia where I grew up, the driest state of the driest inhabited continent in the world. Not that California had ice that was any more natural, but LA was home of the entertainment biz—why let nature get in the way of a good show?

The outdoor rink with its synthetic ice was one of many that had cropped up around the city in honor of the season. A kid in a neon-pink tutu wobbled out onto the slippery surface and went down in a scrambling heap of tulle as soon as she let go of the rail. While my ice-skating experience was minimal, I'd roller-skated plenty of times in my youth and was hoping it wouldn't be too different. All the same, I was glad my outfit wasn't as eye-catching as that tutu.

I looked down at Etta's skates in my lap and their sharp, dangerous-looking blades. I wasn't sure why my septuagenarian neighbor owned a pair since I doubted it was a safe activity for bones that old, but then Etta never prioritized safety. A bit like LA, why let common sense get in the way of a good time?

A glance at my phone told me Connor was late. Connor was rarely late. As if on cue, my phone rang.

"Isobel." Even hearing my name on his lips sent a wave of warmth to my extremities. "I'm sorry, but I'm not going to be able to make our date. Something's come up with one of my security clients. I'll see you tomorrow, okay?"

The laughter and screeching suddenly seemed less merry. "Okay," I said.

He disconnected.

I sat huddled on the bench some more, trying to resurrect my Christmas spirit.

Stuff it.

I didn't need Connor to have fun. I'd go ice-skating without him.

———

MY ALARM WAILED. Who set an alarm on Christmas morning? People who had two hours of travel and just as many hours of agonizing over what to wear ahead of them, that's who.

Meow blinked her sleepy golden-green eyes at me in disapproval. My British housemate Oliver had left yesterday to fly home to see his family, so she'd slept in my room. I petted her dark, striped fur until she closed her eyes again and then swung my legs over the side of the bed. Ouch.

It turned out ice-skating *was* different to roller-skating, and I had the bruises to prove it. Maybe it was good Connor hadn't shown up to witness my humiliation. Except I'd really been looking forward to having some "us time" together, our first as a couple, before the both enthralling and terrifying proposition of meeting his family. On Christmas. No pressure at all.

Briefly I wished I'd stuck to my original plan of spending the day curled up with Meow and a good book, interrupted only by walking Etta's greyhound and Skyping my family back home. Connor's handsome face flashed before me, and my wish dissipated as fast as it had emerged.

What the hell was I going to wear?

Unable to brave such an immense decision without caffeine, I shuffled to the kitchen and made myself a strong cup of tea, wishing as always that it was an espresso coffee instead. Then I shuffled outside onto the stair landing for a few minutes of calm before the day began.

I tripped over a gift basket. After finding a gift-wrapped, severed thumb by my front door just a few days before, I was grateful for the clear cellophane so I could see what was inside. Cookies. My favorite. There was a note attached.

I'm sorry. Fresh start?

I smiled. Connor. He could be sweet under the impassive mask he wore so well. Or maybe Maria, his maid and indispensable assistant, had bossed him into it. I thought about eating one, but I'd baked so many batches of cookies in the past few days (which meant I'd had to sample so many cookies the past few days) that even I was nearing my cookie limit. Plus if I ate any more sugar, I wouldn't fit into half my clothes, and I had enough wardrobe troubles ahead of me.

Of course, clothing didn't play a big part in my evening plans with Connor, but I had to get through the day first.

2

I SURVEYED MYSELF in the mirror and sighed. Why had I said yes?

Okay, I'd been mooning over Connor ever since I found out he had a soul under the hard-ass exterior, and I would've paid to meet his family. If I wasn't so broke, that is.

It was human nature: plunk a box in front of me and tell me I'm not allowed to open it—all I can think about is opening it. So when the man of mystery had invited me in, I would've been hard-pressed to decline even without his sweet, steadfast, and stupidly sexy qualities. But who thought having Christmas with someone's family was a good idea as a first date? It's the thing comedy shows are made of, and I was envisaging disaster upon disaster like *Meet the Parents.*

My heart sped up at the sound of someone knocking on the door. Connor. I hadn't seen him since he'd asked me out two days ago, and my whole body trembled with nerves and anticipation. I braced my knees to hide their shaking, reminding me of the first time we'd met, and opened the door.

His tall, athletic form was backlit by the morning sun, which didn't help my nerves as his gaze swept over me. "Merry Christmas, Isobel."

He would have said, "I found a dead fish, Isobel," in almost the exact same tone.

I stared at his perfect, composed face: the stern dark eyebrows, strong jaw, and warmer-than-usual eyes that offered the only hint he was pleased to see me. Okay, his nose was bruised green from its recent encounter with a walking stick, so he wasn't quite perfect.

I realized I hadn't replied. "Merry—"

The rest of the sentence and everything else fled from my brain as he leaned down, cupped my head in both hands, and kissed me thoroughly. "I've been looking forward to that," he murmured, voice and breath soft against my cheek.

I didn't say anything since my brain was malfunctioning. Maybe if I'd had that coffee . . .

"Are you ready?" he asked. "Or should I bring your coffee up from the car?"

Once again, I had let the silence drag out for too long. I'd been imagining dragging him into my bedroom—in spite of my secondhand duvet cover, which looked like a rainbow with a nasty stomach bug—and arriving at his family lunch late, but decidedly more merry.

I blinked and snapped out of my fantasy. "Ah, sure I am. Let me grab my things."

Connor had banned me from buying any gifts, so I'd made a traditional Australian dessert, pavlova, and a plate of gingerbread man cookies to contribute. However, when I'd gone to pack the gingerbread men, I'd discovered my thieving weasel of a housemate Oliver had stolen them for his plane trip. Either that or they'd used their little legs to run, run away as fast as they could. So now I was bringing a plate of the cookies Connor had gifted me this morning instead.

I gave Meow a last cuddle for courage, grabbed the desserts and my bag, and walked with my hot date to his SUV.

———

I STARED AT THE PASSING desert landscape and reflected that today might just turn out to be my worst Christmas ever.

"Are we there yet?" I asked.

Not even the suggestion of a smile brushed Connor's lips. "No."

The familiar hum of the engine was the only sound. The only sound for most of the past hour I'd spent in the car with my new romantic partner.

It wasn't very romantic. It was more like driving with the Grinch.

We couldn't agree on music. He liked classical, I liked indie rock. I'd suggested Christmas carols since it was, after all, Christmas morning, but he'd declined those too. "Some of them are classics," I'd argued. He'd driven on without bothering to answer. The relentless noise of the engine seemed to rise in volume as I wondered again whether I'd made a terrible mistake.

"That was a joke," I pointed out. "About whether we're there yet."

He didn't say anything, but I could guess what went through his head. *Not a very good one.*

It was true. I couldn't even win an argument in my imaginary conversation with Connor.

I looked at his profile again. Drop-dead gorgeous. But this car trip was turning out to be drop-dead boring. And eerily similar to the one to Porterville three and a half months ago. We had just found out that Albert Alstrom, a celebrity chef and our primary lead in a poisoning case, was a dead end and had desperately needed new information on the case. Hence the road trip to talk to a potential witness. But at the time, I'd been certain Connor could barely tolerate me. It hadn't been a fun drive.

This time was different though, I reminded myself. My fingers drummed the section of the door panel that served as an armrest. He'd told me he admired me. That he found me refreshing. Called me *warm* and *genuine*. Sure, he'd called me *impossible* and *hardheaded* as well, but he said he wanted to see me more often. It was his idea to bring me to his family Christmas. So why the heck was he stonewalling me?

Was it my choice of clothing? I looked down at the T-shirt Oliver had gifted me for Christmas. It featured two cartoon gingerbread men, one with a bite taken out of his leg, saying, "I can't feel my leg," and the other with a bite out of his head saying, "What?"

I'd agonized all morning over what to wear. To give the right impression. But the impression I wanted to give Connor: stupendously sexy, and the impression I wanted to give his family: intelligent and responsible, were at odds with each other. In the end, I'd given up and worn Oliver's gift and a pair of jeans. Sometimes it's better not to try too hard than to try hard and miss the mark. Besides, when else was I going to wear the T-shirt?

But the jeans were another mistake. Who's dumb enough to wear too-tight jeans to an eating occasion like Christmas?

Especially when eating might be a much-needed way of avoiding conversation and consoling myself.

"Is something wrong?" I asked Connor, trying to kick my mind out of its spiral of doom.

"No." He glanced over at me. "Of course not."

"Then why are we just sitting here in silence? Shouldn't we be, I don't know, deep in conversation, learning things about each other?"

I was the kind of girl who was usually comfortable with silence, but I'd been hoping for a little more feel-good conversation on my first date and first Christmas away from home.

Connor looked my way again, and I saw the slightest crease at the corners of his eyes, indicating he was amused. "I already know an awful lot about you, Isobel Matilda Avery. And besides, I like silence."

My fingers abruptly ceased their drumming. I hated my middle name. I'd heard enough colorful renditions of the Australian ballad "Waltzing Matilda" to be scarred for life. No way had I ever used it around him.

Then I remembered: he'd read my file. "That's not fair." We both worked for the same company protecting high-end clients, which was how we met. But he was an investigator, and I was a highly specialized poison taster. "You should let me see your file to level the playing field," I said, knowing it would never happen. Both our jobs were strictly classified, and our employer operated on a need-to-know basis.

"I'm afraid that's against Taste Society policy." His tone hadn't changed, but my gut told me he was gleeful about the policy.

"Then at least tell me about your family."

"You'll meet them yourself in another hour."

I restrained myself from throwing my hands in the air. I knew from experience he only got more uncommunicative in the face of emotion. This was not going well. And I was about to be introduced to his mom and his sister, two people I intuitively knew he valued above anyone else. What if they were just like him? It would be the most stilted Christmas ever. Maybe I'd leave having said nothing other than "nice to meet you" and "pass the wine." I definitely chose the wrong outfit too. I needed to go to my happy place.

"Well, if we can't talk and we can't listen to music, can we get something to eat?"

This time, his lips twitched. "You realize we're going there to have lunch, right?"

I refused to rise to the bait. My appetite was a constant source of amusement for him, but I'd skipped breakfast in a misguided attempt to fit into my jeans, and I couldn't cope with any more of this on an empty stomach. "I'm sure I'll be hungry again by then."

His shoulders dropped a quarter inch, conceding the point. "Where do you want to go?"

"Whatever we come across next will be fine. But skip the drive-through and get a park."

"Need to stretch your legs?" he asked.

I shot him a dirty look. "No. I'm just making sure you don't put sleeping drugs in my food again."

That was how he'd dealt with my unwanted attempts at conversation on our last road trip.

3

AS I LEFT THE SAFETY of the SUV and walked to Connor's mother's home, I thought perhaps I should've written a letter to Santa telling him all I wanted for Christmas was for this lunch to go okay. If I'd posted it express, it might have gotten there in time.

The home itself was a cute 1900s cottage with a generous A-frame roof, painted a chirpy white. It was set back from the road by a long driveway and nestled amongst a well-tended garden. Beyond the garden were towering oak trees on gently sloping, grassy land that seemed to typify this corner of San Bernardino County.

Despite the peace of the picturesque scene, adrenaline pumped through my veins for the second time today.

What if they hated me? Connor hadn't liked me at first. My mind flashed back to the destination of our last road trip, and I decided I'd rather be facing that gang of turkeys. And I *really* don't like turkeys. Except dead, naked, and trussed on the dinner table anyway.

A woman in her fifties came out the front door and down the steps. I couldn't see much of Connor in her, except for the stern nose and cleft chin. She was followed by an exuberant German shorthaired pointer who raced over and planted two paws on my stomach, giving me an excuse to postpone the moment of our official meeting.

"Agatha, down!" the woman reprimanded. "Connor, why didn't you tell us you were bringing someone?"

My hands froze in rewarding Agatha for her naughty behavior, and I gaped at Connor incredulously.

He raised an eyebrow a fraction. "Don't," he said.

I snapped my jaw shut, thinking he was talking to me.

His mother shot me a smile. "Don't worry, dear, I'm just teasing." She pulled me into a hug, then stepped back to look at me. "I'll have you know that Connor didn't get his lack of humor from me. We're delighted to have you. Do you have any idea how long it's been since he brought a girl home to our little family?"

"Don't," Connor warned again.

Her dark eyes glinted with mischief. "Gosh. He must have still been in diapers."

It took a moment for my brain to catch up. "Just how long did it take him to graduate from diapers?" I asked.

She clapped me on the shoulder and laughed. "Oh, thank goodness, I was worried you'd be a stickler like him."

Connor looked at us both with resignation. "Isobel, meet my mother, Mae."

———

TEN MINUTES LATER, I'd been introduced to his sister, Harper, as well, and we were all squeezed into the tiny cottage kitchen. Agatha had opted to lie in the middle of the tiles in everyone's way.

I watched the man next to me do up the ties of his Rudolph the Reindeer apron and thought—not for the first time—that I'd known more about complete strangers after ten minutes of small talk than I did about my date. My eyes flicked to my own cartoon T-shirt. When I'd decided to wear it this morning, I would have never in my wildest dreams expected to match the oh-so-suave Connor. Of course, under the apron he was wearing his usual tailored shirt and jeans.

I smirked at him. "You look good in Christmas cartoons."

"I always look good," he said without missing a beat.

His sister pulled a face and smacked a rolling pin into

his hands. "You're always an idiot too. Don't you know you're supposed to return the compliment? Now get rolling."

Harper's apron depicted a plump Santa in a distressing state of undress. Beneath it, she was tall, lean, and muscular, like her brother. As a mechanic, her muscles no doubt came in handy. Her hair was the same rich espresso brown as her brother's too, but where his gray eyes were frequently cold and flinty, hers sparkled like the baubles on the Christmas tree. They lit on me now. "Are you sure you'll be able to put up with him?" she asked.

"Absolutely not," I said. "Do you have any tips?"

Connor had moved to the pizza dough Harper had just finished kneading. We were apparently having Christmas pizzas for lunch.

She flashed me a wicked grin. "It all comes down to finding creative ways to annoy him."

Maybe this wouldn't be such a disaster after all . . .

————

I SURREPTITIOUSLY unfastened the top button of my jeans and leaned to the left like the ancient Romans used to do after they'd overindulged. The position was supposed to relieve the pressure on your stomach. I was stuffed, and we hadn't even started on dessert.

Once again, they insisted I serve myself first. In addition to the pavlova with berries and cream and the cookies that I'd contributed, there were peppermint chocolate brownies, a pumpkin pie, and a gingerbread cheesecake. I loaded up my plate with a tiny portion of each and tried to decide where to start. The cookie perhaps. I was curious about what flavor Connor would've chosen for me.

I sampled a piece, testing for poison out of habit. The decadent tones of butter and rum rolled over my tongue first, followed by cinnamon, nutmeg, cloves, and . . .

Crap.

Chloral hydrate. I spat the soggy crumbs into my napkin. What the hell had Connor been thinking? A prank probably, meant just for me who was trained to taste it. Chloral hydrate was a central nervous system depressant used as a sleeping aid or, in larger doses, unconsciousness and death. Maybe he'd thought I'd try a cookie before we drove here and be amused by the reminder of our last road trip. But how could he have allowed me to serve them to his family? On Christmas? Especially seeing as mixing chloral hydrate with alcohol made it a lot more dangerous. The rum alone might not be enough to do it, but we'd all been drinking wine as well. Was it possible Connor hadn't known about the alcohol thing?

I watched in horror as Connor's mom picked up one of the cookies.

If I didn't say anything, it was probable that nobody would die thanks to the small dose, but it would definitely ruin Christmas. If I did say something, I'd blow my cover, break my Taste Society oath, and blow up years of Connor's deception. No one was allowed to know the truth of our jobs. Including family.

Mae raised the cookie to take her first bite. I had to stop her. Give myself time to think.

I leapt to my feet, startling everyone and the dog. "I'd, uh, like to propose a toast," I announced, grabbing my wineglass and making it up as I went along. "You guys have welcomed me like I'm family, and I really appreciate it." My brain raced frantically. Connor's mom had picked up her wineglass but was still holding the cookie in her other hand. "Um, I thought I'd be alone today, missing my loved ones back in Australia. I would've had Meow for company, of course. Uh, that's my housemate's cat. Long story. But never mind that, the point I'm trying to make is, well, thank you." Everyone was waiting to hear the actual toast part of the toast: Mae smiling sympathetically, Harper trying not to laugh. Agatha looked like she wanted to hear more about the cat. "So, here's to family and to Christmas."

"To family and to Christmas," they all repeated. Except for Agatha, whose attention had shifted back to the food.

Connor was regarding me with a perplexed look that only made me madder. I wasn't going to forgive him for this.

My hand trembled as I met his eye and thrust the glass into his as hard as I could. I was envisaging it shattering, sending a shower of glass and wine onto the cookies. Instead, he saw my glass coming too fast and reacted to soften the collision. Half my wine sloshed over the rim onto Connor's arm. It served him right, but that left less liquid to drown the cookies in. Thinking quickly, I dropped my glass on top of them. I was seconds too late for it to look like reflex, but I had to hope no one else would notice.

"Oh my gosh, I'm so sorry! What a klutz I am." I gave a tremulous smile, wishing I could disappear. In part so I could be alone with my mortification and in part so I could use my invisibility to gain the upper hand in kicking Connor's ass.

His mom put her cookie down and hurried to get a cloth to clean up the spillage. I made as if to follow her, then snatched the unspoiled cookie from her plate and stuffed it into my jeans pocket. With my jeans already too tight, it was going to make an awful mess, but I couldn't ditch it under the table or Agatha would eat it.

I looked down to check there were no telltale crumbs to give away my hiding place. It was then I remembered my pants were undone.

4

FEIGNING THAT nothing was wrong and keeping up with the banter over dessert, tea, and coffee was nearly impossible. Acting had never been my strong suit. By the time we walked back to the SUV, I was ready to burst. I still couldn't believe what Connor had almost allowed to happen.

I turned on him as soon as we'd waved goodbye and were out of sight. "How the hell could you?"

"What?"

"You know exactly what. Don't play with me."

"I have no idea what you're talking about."

I considered digging the mutilated cookie out of my pocket and throwing it at him. Instead, I continued my rant. "Enough. It wasn't funny from the moment you let me serve poisoned cookies to your family, and it sure as heck isn't funny now!"

His voice was quiet, a stark contrast from my own. "Start at the beginning."

I was going to keep yelling, but for all his faults, Connor wasn't one to deny being a jerk. And he didn't look amused. Not in the least. In fact, he looked a bit scary.

"The cookies?" I prompted.

Nothing.

"That you sent me this morning?"

Still nothing.

"As an apology for missing our date yesterday?"

"I didn't send you any cookies," Connor said.

"Oh." Weird that a part of me was disappointed he hadn't sent me cookies. Especially when they'd turned out to be poisoned, but there it was. "Then who did?"

"No idea, but if they were poisoned, I'll be damned if I let them get away with it."

All hint of the man who'd cupped my head in his hands and kissed my brains out this morning was gone. I felt another pang of disappointment since I'd been hoping that I'd see more of that man tonight. But there was no chance of it now. He'd switched into professional PI mode.

"Tell me everything. When, where, and how did you get them? What were they poisoned with?"

It's not that I didn't want him to have my back. I loved that about him. It was only that this evening, I wanted him to have my front as well.

"Can't this wait until tomorrow?" I asked. Now that I knew he wasn't behind the "prank," I really, *really* wanted to go ahead with my original plans.

Connor didn't answer, just looked at me.

I slumped down in my seat and started talking.

———

I WAS GRATEFUL TO CONCLUDE the pool of people who might send me poisoned cookies was not large. In fact, ruling out my current date's possible idea of a prank and my ex-husband due to his lack of poisoning knowledge, I could only think of one.

Albert Alstrom. The celebrity chef who'd become scarily fixated on me after I'd played the star-struck fan as part of an investigation. We'd ruled him out as the person behind the murder attempt but learned he had no qualms about using date rape drugs to get his women to cooperate. When I still didn't cooperate, he upped the game by poisoning Meow and then me as well.

Lucky for the bastard that Meow hadn't suffered any lasting harm, or he might not have gone to jail with all of his body parts.

The jail was where we were heading now, despite my protests.

I had a feeling Albert would enjoy a Christmas visit from me all too much. And I still thought that since the threat was already minimized, the damn case could wait till tomorrow.

Connor had other priorities.

Maybe if I made a move on him, I could convince him to change those priorities, but what if it wasn't enough to change them? What if he brushed me off? My confidence wasn't high enough to take the risk. Especially in my stupid cartoon T-shirt.

I let a sigh escape. Hopefully Albert would admit to doing it, Connor would feel like he'd protected me, and then we could spend some time together, for the first time in our entire relationship, doing something other than working a case.

Albert had managed to weasel his way into Seal Beach's pay-to-stay jail program for nonviolent, affluent offenders. It was his first conviction, and since I'd escaped before he could do anything (and some might add because he had the status and wealth of a celebrity), he'd gotten off lightly. The jail offered relative luxury confinement compared to the county prison, but as I followed Connor's broad shoulders down the narrow corridor, I was glad to see it was a major step down from Albert's mansion in Bel Air.

I was also glad for Connor's strength and quiet competence. Despite logic telling me I had nothing to worry about, my palms were damp. I wiped them on my jeans.

We entered the crowded visitors' area. Crowded because of Christmas, I guessed. Albert was waiting for us in an orange jumpsuit. It was not his color, and without the benefits of a stylish haircut and tailored clothes, he reminded me more of the kid who'd been bullied in school than the successful, scheming celebrity. Even so, as his pale blue eyes stalked me across the room, I found myself wiping my hands on my jeans again.

"Isobel!" he practically sang, the goofy grin I remembered making an appearance. It was a grin that might put you at ease if you didn't know better. "I'm so glad to see you. Wow. I never expected this. A visit on Christmas? How blessed am I? I mean, I know Christmas is a time for second chances and all, but I never thought you'd forgive me."

He was acting weird. Usually he'd be trying to play it cool. Trying to impress me. Trying to act like he had more power than he did. Now he was like a little kid presented with ice cream.

"What the hell makes you think she'd forgive you?" Connor cut in.

Albert jumped as if he hadn't noticed Connor's existence. "The cookies. You got them, didn't you?"

Connor's knuckles whitened. "So you did send them, you little shit."

Albert raised his hands, revealing the long, slender fingers that I'd always found creepy. "Hey, man. There's no need for jealousy. I wasn't trying to make a move or anything. I only wanted her to know I was sorry for what I did." Albert's focus returned to me. "Didn't you get the note? 'I'm sorry. Fresh start?' I've joined the Brotherhood of the Enlightened Path and I've been transformed. One of the steps to ascension is to go back and try to make amends with everyone you've hurt. Of course I couldn't visit you"—he gave a self-deprecating shrug—"but I wanted to do something."

I shook my head. "Albert, the cookies were poisoned."

"What? No way! I swear on all my awards and accolades they were a genuine apology. I was trying to make amends. I'm a different person now. Really."

I was starting to believe him. Sadly, his own achievements were probably the most important thing in his life. Plus, his attention hadn't strayed once to my chest or my crotch; his former favorite places to look.

"Then why didn't you sign the note?" I asked.

"I didn't? I mean, George, my butler should've signed it from me. But then how did you know they were from me?"

I mustered the courage to meet his eyes. Eyes I'd had nightmares about after what he'd done, or tried to do, to me. "Because they were poisoned."

"Oh." He looked genuinely crestfallen. "I . . . Well, I don't know what to tell you. I swear they weren't meant to be poisoned."

Connor cracked his knuckles. "Who else had access to the cookies? How did you arrange the delivery?"

"George made them from an old recipe of mine. I couldn't send her the store-bought variety, could I? He was supposed to deliver them as well, but I guess he might have paid someone to do it . . ."

"Give us his details."

Albert recited them and wrote a note to George requesting full cooperation. Then he looked at me anxiously. "I know it's a lot to ask, but would you maybe tell me when you've got this figured out? I'd hate to go on thinking that my peace offering had caused you further harm."

Connor pushed off the table and stood up. "We'll think about it." Then he ushered me out, shielding me from Albert's gaze as we left the jail.

5

IT TURNED OUT that after Albert had become "enlightened," he'd invited George and his family to move in to his Bel Air mansion while he was away. He'd already been paying the butler to upkeep it in his absence, so it was more convenient for George to live on-site.

We passed through the ten-foot security fence and walked up to the bright blue door. The building was made of two rectangular prisms set atop one another and cantilevered at a forty-five-degree angle, like the toy blocks of a giant child. Floor-to-ceiling dark windows contrasted with the smooth white walls. Beautiful but comfortless, the way I remembered.

I almost expected George to answer the door in a tux as he had the last time I stood on the doorstep, but of course, even perfect English butlers didn't play butler to their own families on Christmas. He was wearing the bottom half of a Santa suit and a T-shirt that said "World's Greatest Dad."

Regardless of his outfit, he still had his hauteur. He looked down his long nose at me, unhappy recognition on his face. "Ms. Avery. To what do I owe the pleasure of your company on this special day?" His tone was faultlessly polite yet somehow managed to convey that it was very rude of me to interrupt the aforementioned special day.

Connor flashed his PI credentials. "We have a few questions. Did Mr. Alstrom ask you to make and deliver cookies to Ms. Avery?"

"May I enquire as to what this is about?"

Connor handed him the note Albert had written.

"Yes, he did," George confirmed after perusing it with care.

"Be specific. What did he ask you to do?"

"To make cookies for Ms. Avery, following his recipe exactly. He was very particular on that point, as he always is about anything food related. Then he dictated a note for me to attach to the gift and asked me to deliver it so she'd get it on Christmas."

"Did you do as he instructed? And did you deliver them yourself?"

"Of course."

"Why did you leave them outside rather than delivering them in person?"

"Mr. Alstrom only made his request last night, and it was too late to knock by the time I finished baking them, but I had to deliver them yesterday because I had other commitments today."

I wasn't imagining the double layer of meaning George gave to the reminder that he "had other commitments today." He wasn't pleased by our intrusion.

Connor either didn't pick up on it or didn't care. Probably both. "Then do you have any idea how they ended up containing the drug chloral hydrate?"

George's tone became more haughty. "I most certainly do not. I don't even know what that is."

"Where did you cook them?

"In Mr. Alstrom's kitchen."

"Is that where you normally cook?"

"No. We have a separate kitchen, but Mr. Alstrom wanted me to use his for the cookies. He was particular about that kind of thing, as I said."

"We'd like to see the ingredients you used."

George let out a sigh. "If you must."

I figured there would be rules against sighing along with any other visible form of exasperation in butler school. George was slipping. Maybe because he'd had no one to serve for three months.

Granting us entrance, he escorted us the exceedingly long distance to the kitchen. Although with Connor by my side and a more sensible choice of shoes, it felt less long this time.

Albert's glossy black and stainless steel kitchen was a mess. As if sensing my thoughts, George said, "I planned to clean it up tomorrow. It was terribly late by the time I'd finished, and I still needed to help my wife wrap presents and finish cooking our own Christmas meals. Which reminds me, my daughters are getting ready for bed and won't want to go to sleep without me saying goodnight. May I leave you here for a few minutes?"

"Are the ingredients you used on the bench?"

"A lot of them are, and the recipe I followed is there too."

"All right. Say goodnight to your daughters."

The rum was worth $200 a bottle. The spices had been bought fresh from the Santa Monica Farmers Market, their flavors preserved by vacuum-sealed jars. The vanilla beans were plump and juicy, the sugar the expensive coconut variety, and the butter the real deal, homemade from organic cream. The cornstarch and all-purpose flour were . . . well, cornstarch and all-purpose flour, but not the generic-brand kind that stocked my own shelves. The self-rising flour was missing. After I'd tasted everything and found no trace of chloral hydrate in any of them, we found an empty packet of self-rising flour in the trash can.

Grudgingly I pulled it out and searched for a clean sample in the crinkled paper. Connor waited expectantly.

"Clear," I said, feeling defeated. Every failure to identify the poisoner led me further and further from my former plans for the evening. "So I guess that means someone poisoned them after they'd been delivered?"

"Or Alstrom is lying, has already covered his tracks, and organized George to waste our time," Connor pointed out.

I brushed a weary hand over my face before remembering it had just been in the trash can. "But he seemed so upset about it."

"That's the clever thing to do if he's lying. He's probably bored out of his brain in prison, and the old Alstrom would've delighted in the elaborate ruse. Either that or it's George who's lying."

"Why would *he* want to poison me though? I never did anything to him."

"It most likely isn't about you at all. Think about it. He's living in this mansion and getting paid for it, with nothing to do except maintain the place and fulfill Alstrom's occasional request from jail."

"So he's trying to extend Albert's sentence?"

"Exactly."

"Then why wouldn't he claim Albert told him to poison the cookies?"

"Because Albert has control of his assets despite being

in prison. He'd kick George out."

I shook my head in disbelief. "So I get poisoned on Christmas to save George from having to go back to working for a living?"

"Maybe. Let's ask him."

"WHY DIDN'T you sign Albert's name on the note?" Connor asked.

George had changed out of the bottom half of his Santa suit but was still wearing the "World's Greatest Dad" T-shirt.

"Mr. Alstrom didn't ask me to," he said. "I wrote exactly what he instructed."

"And he didn't mention how to sign it?"

"No. I assumed he wanted it to be anonymous."

Sounded plausible enough. Which wouldn't help us convince George to reveal his secret.

Connor tapped the recipe on the kitchen counter. "You said you followed this recipe to the letter, right?"

"That's correct."

I looked over the recipe again, wondering if we could've missed an ingredient. Then it struck me.

"Then where's the rest of the self-rising flour?" I asked.

"What do you mean?"

"Do you expect us to believe that you had the exact, perfect amount of one and a quarter cups of self-rising flour left in that packet in the trash can? I've been baking for years, and that *never* happens."

George shook his head, but Connor jumped in with his own observation. "Before you answer, it didn't escape our notice that all of Albert's ingredients are stored in canisters. The packet in the trash was the only one we found."

The butler's eyes flicked back and forth between us in disbelief. "Did Mr. Alstrom put you up to this? How did he find out?"

Connor leaned in, doing the menacing bluff he did so well. "Tell us the truth."

George didn't shrink away from Connor. Years of dealing with the powerful meant he stood straight and composed as he answered.

"The truth is Mr. Alstrom rang me at eleven p.m. on Christmas Eve and told me he'd come up with a great idea. He proceeded to outline how I was to make cookies to his specifications and deliver them to Ms. Avery for Christmas. Let me reiterate that it was eleven p.m. Christmas Eve. Of course I started doing as he asked regardless. But when I found out there was no self-rising flour and then learned my wife had finished almost all ours too, something came over me. Frankly, it wasn't worth the nuisance of going to the shops on Christmas Eve and waiting in line for an hour on the casual whim of my employer for an ingredient that didn't matter anyway. So I used the last of the self-rising flour my wife had and swapped the rest for all-purpose flour, baking powder, and salt like any normal person would do."

Connor was already fishing them out of the cupboards. "This baking powder and salt?"

"Yes." Now that Connor had walked away, George had allowed his posture to wilt. "Please don't tell Mr. Alstrom. I'm not sure how deep the new reformed version of him runs. Especially when it comes to cooking."

I tasted the salt. Clear. Then the baking powder.

It wasn't baking powder. The label clearly said baking powder, but it was chloral hydrate, hidden in plain sight. No wonder Albert was particular about using the right ingredients if this is where he stocked all his illicit substances. And from what I knew of the unreformed Albert, I doubted George was aware of the practice.

Which meant the whole fiasco was a comedy of errors. Albert really had wanted to apologize with a delicious gift. George really had innocently dosed the cookies with chloral hydrate—due to wanting to save himself a trip to the shops and his employer's deliberate mislabeling. And my housemate had not so innocently stolen the gingerbread men I'd prepared. All of which had led me to bringing the untasted poisoned cookies to Connor's family Christmas lunch.

I closed the lid carefully and tugged Connor's sleeve. "Thanks for your honesty, George. We'll be taking the baking powder with us." A moment later, I grabbed the homemade butter. "This too."

6

I THOUGHT ABOUT SENDING a note to Albert to let him know it had been a misunderstanding, but I couldn't work out how to suggest he throw out all his mis-labeled ingredients as part of his reform without getting George in trouble. I leaned my head against the car window and decided it could wait until tomorrow. I'd wasted enough time on Albert today.

Connor must have seen me use the glass as a pillow. "It's been a long day. I'll drop you home."

"I'd prefer it if you didn't just *drop* me home," I told him.

"Of course. I'll walk you to your door and make sure there aren't any other nasty surprises waiting for you."

I rolled my head against the glass so I could see his face. "I was hoping you might walk me farther than that.

Like, to my bedroom. Or yours preferably since your bed is bigger than mine." That and his duvet cover was less embarrassing.

His eyes widened. "Oh . . ."

"For an intelligent man who deduces things for a living, you can be rather slow sometimes."

Connor pulled the car to a sudden stop. We were on a quiet suburban street with only the light cast by streetlamps to see by. He studied me hungrily for long tense seconds before trailing his fingertips across my cheek, down my neck, and along the length of my arm. Then he captured my hand in his and raised it to his lips.

By the time he was done demonstrating his talent on my fingers, my body had caught fire and my awareness had narrowed to his skin on mine.

He drew me closer, his muscled arm supporting my back as he leaned in to meet me.

"Yes, Isobel," he said, his breath tickling my ear. "Tonight I'll show you just how slow I can be . . ."

POISON
IS THE NEW
BLACK

1

HER HAIR WAS the color of Snow White's poisoned apple, her lips painted to match. She used those lips to smile sweetly at me and clasped her hands in her lap. "I've never met a Shade before. What a quaint little thing you are. You must be so brave to put your life on the line for perfect strangers."

Blue eyes assessed me. Wondering whether I'd read between the lines. Wondering how I'd react.

I read between the lines just fine. She thought I looked like an uncultured bumpkin, and she wasn't pleased about it. The brave comment was to remind me who held the power in this relationship. If I'd been born naturally brave, I wouldn't have wasted the virtue on protecting the rich and famous. There was only one reason for me to take this job: money. And my potential client had me pegged. Whoever had the money had the power, and she had loads of it.

"I'm pleased to offer you a new experience, ma'am," I said, matching her saccharine tone.

Those eyes narrowed. She didn't appreciate the reminder of our age gap. Considering her wealth, designer clothes, and the best face and body modern medicine could offer, it was the one thing I had going for me.

"Call me Mrs. Madison. I insist," she said with emphasis on the insist part.

"Of course, Mrs. Madison."

She let her hands fall apart and then folded them together again. We were sitting in a parlor, the type that only exists in houses with more rooms than anyone knows what to do with. It was a pretty place to be judged wanting, with a large open fireplace and three arched windows edged with soft, gauzy curtains. The ornate, solid-timber furnishings paired with their pale luxury fabrics were chosen to demonstrate money and taste. At least Vanessa Madison had both. Money was a given in the glamorous western district of Los Angeles, but style was a rarer commodity.

"I thought the Taste Society would send someone with more polish for this role," she told me. "The Westside Elite

Charity and Social Club can be vicious, and you'll need to withstand intense scrutiny."

Vanessa Madison was president of the Westside Elite Charity and Social (WECS) Club, and it was the other members she needed protection from. But she didn't need the type of protection a normal bodyguard could provide—threatening someone that way would be tactless. The rich and famous had their own, more subtle, weapon of choice. Which was where Shades like me came in—to protect them from sabotage and murder attempts of the poison variety.

"That won't be a problem," I lied. Acting wasn't exactly a strength of mine, but I was learning to bluff with the best of them.

"And you're so pale. As my dietary adviser, shouldn't you look more healthy?"

She was evaluating me as if I were an animal on the auction block, and I wondered if she'd want to check my teeth and gums.

With great restraint, I resisted baring them at her. "I have extensive food and catering experience that will be an asset to the role," I said instead.

It was a stretch of the truth, but that's what you did in job interviews. Not that I was sure I wanted the job anymore. It had looked good on paper: a client I only had to attend at public functions rather than around-the-clock protection; a low risk of lethal substances; and a cover story that gave me no need to feign an intimate relationship. I should've known it was too good to be true.

Vanessa Madison might just be my most terrifying client yet.

"Well, all right then." She cocked her head, her glossy red hair gliding over her shoulders as if it were starring in a shampoo commercial. "I suppose if you don't work out, I can always fire you and get a new one."

———

CONNOR STILES, a fellow Taste Society agent and now my boyfriend, was waiting for me outside in his SUV. While I stopped clients from being poisoned, he investigated who was behind the attempts. He also assessed new Shade recruits, which was how we'd met.

The romantic side of our relationship was just days old, and I wasn't entirely sure how we'd ended up together. At first glance, with his tailored clothes and striking good looks, he seemed a much better fit for Vanessa Madison.

But he'd had plenty of opportunities to mingle with the Vanessa Madisons of this world, and he'd chosen me: an almost-thirty-year-old Australian who knew nothing about fashion, cared even less, and was still trying to get her life in order.

Of course, it had taken months for him to warm to me.

"How'd it go?" he asked now.

I hoisted myself into my seat and blew some stray hair out of my eyes. "Remember our first meeting?"

One eyebrow went up a fraction. "That bad, huh?"

"Worse," I said.

His hand found mine and caressed it in a way that stirred the slumbering beast that was my libido. It had been in hibernation for the past two years until Connor and I had woken it up big time last night. And like any newly awakened beast, it had a hunger that wouldn't be satiated anytime soon.

"Do you need cheering up?" he asked, leaning in and pressing his lips to the underside of my jaw.

"Uh-huh." My agreement came out soft and breathy.

He started the engine. "Then let's get coffee and comfort food. I'll cheer you up some more after that."

I snapped on my seat belt and shot him a grin. "You know me so well."

Thirty minutes later, we were sipping our matching espressos, and I was polishing off the last of my carrot cake. We were in a cute little café with views over the foothills of West LA. Connor had chosen the spot because he knew I missed the sense of space and natural vistas I'd grown up with in the Adelaide Hills, Australia.

I stared at the handsome face in front of me and marveled at how lovely it was to share my favorite drink with a man who cared for me. Not just pretended to care for me. Cared for me.

He caught me staring, and his lips curved upward. We were a long way from being truly familiar with each other, but the muscles in his face were relaxed out of its usual impassive mask, and I didn't take the compliment lightly.

"Are you ready for round two of mission cheer up?" he asked.

I scooped up the last bit of cream cheese frosting and popped it into my mouth suggestively. "Can't wait."

2

I FELL BACK onto the soft linen, feeling relaxed and loose-limbed with contentment in a way I hadn't experienced in eons. Connor was extremely talented at satisfying my physical needs. Both in my stomach and in the bedroom.

"That was amazing," I breathed.

Connor grunted in a way that said, "Well, duh."

The art of communication was something we were working on.

I took another minute to revel in my happy afterglow before rolling to face him. His almost-buzz-cut-length hair meant it was still perfect, while my unruly, red-brown mop probably looked like a troop of monkeys had been pawing through it searching for bugs. His gray eyes were on me. Hopefully not focused on my hair. And the lips, which were usually set in a determined line, were soft for once. Even vulnerable.

I tried again. "So tell me something about yourself that I don't know."

"There's nothing to tell."

"We're both aware that's not true."

Although I'd known him for four months, I'd learned very little about him outside the cases we'd worked on together. Here's what I did know: he always protected me, always had my back, and was always there for me when I needed him. He just didn't often have the words to tell me so.

Since my ex-husband had the words without the action bit, I knew which was more important.

And yesterday I'd met Connor's family over Christmas lunch. An honor that said a lot about how much he trusted me. But aside from that, the sole time he'd given me a glimpse into his personal life was to make me feel better after a distressful encounter with severed body parts.

I guess he figured he'd done enough to make me feel better today after my meeting with Vanessa Madison because he stayed silent.

"Well, what's happening at work at the moment?" I asked, thinking it might be easier for him to chat about something less personal. He wasn't a big talker, so maybe we needed to start small.

"It's classified," he said.

That was true. Everything with our employer was classified. "Not the Taste Society stuff. Your other security stuff."

"That's classified too."

"Can't you speak about it in general terms, without mentioning specifics?"

He grunted again. This one I took to mean, "Yes, but I don't want to."

I sighed, and this one wasn't quite as contented as my last. "How are we going to find things to talk about if all of your current life is classified and you don't want to talk about your past?"

I guess what I was really wondering was when would he let me past his defenses? If he never did, then he'd always be there for me, and I would just be there. Useless. I wanted to be able to help him the way he helped me.

"Talking is overrated." His hand crept lower again to emphasize his point, and my breath caught.

"Even if you are some kind of demigod who's ready to go again already, at some point we'll need to do something other than food and sex. What then?"

His hand hadn't stopped, lazily spiraling lower and lower. "Then we'll figure something out," he said.

For a while, I didn't ask him any more questions.

When I was once again sprawled out on the soft linen, I tried again. "So when you said you wanted to spend more time with me, was this all you had in mind?"

Connor slid out of bed and stretched his gloriously naked form before me. "You seemed to be enjoying yourself."

Unlike me, he had no inhibitions about his body.

I flushed. "Careful, schnookums, or I'll have to take Harper's advice and concoct creative ways of annoying you." Harper was his sister whom I'd recently had the pleasure of meeting.

He paused on his way to the shower, not having the decency to show so much as a flicker of annoyance at my carefully-chosen-to-irritate pet name. "That reminds me, she wants to see you. Is it okay if I give her your number?"

"Sure. But why is it that your sister would like to have a conversation with me when you don't?"

"Because my sister doesn't have the option of doing what we just did together." His gaze raked over my figure, which was only half covered by the sheets. "Want to join me in the shower?"

"Are you serious? I don't think my legs could hold me."

He gave me a smug smile. "That won't be a problem."

———

HOURS LATER, I drove my beautiful company car—a middle-aged silver Corvette—to my apartment building in Palms and hurried up the two flights of external stairs. I had forty-five minutes to make myself presentable for tonight's WECS Club function. It wasn't going to be enough. But today had been a rare chance for Connor and I to spend a lazy afternoon together, and I'd wanted to make the most of it.

At least I'd showered already.

I crossed the third-floor stair landing and waved at the security camera Connor had installed this morning. It was his response to a couple of nasty gifts that had been left by my front door in the past week. Probably no one was monitoring the live camera feed, but waving made me feel less weird about the possibility.

I had to avert my eyes from Santa's bared butt cheeks as I unlocked the door. My housemate had decided a poster featuring the aforementioned butt cheeks with bright red letters spelling Merry Chrismyass was an improvement over the traditional wreaths. Christmas was now behind us (no pun intended), and today was Boxing Day, but I hadn't found time to remove it yet. It would have to stay up awhile longer.

Inside, the apartment was quiet. My housemate was in England visiting his family for the holiday season, so it was just me and his cat Meow. The place we called home was run-down and tacky compared to my new client or boyfriend's grand residences. It had been built in the 1960s and retained the original kitchen, bathroom, and much of the flooring. Our mishmash of preloved furniture didn't help. But the price was right, the neighborhood was safe, and the company was first-rate.

I'd picked Meow up for a cuddle when Etta, my favorite neighbor, pushed through the door behind me.

"Isobel. We need to talk."

She never called me Isobel anymore. My friends and family called me Izzy. Except when they were about to broach an uncomfortable topic or give me a lecture. This didn't bode well.

"I'm sorry, but I'm in a hurry. Can this wait?"

"No. It can't. The time has come for me to tell you something. Something you're not gonna like much, I'm afraid. You might want to sit down."

I looked her over. As usual, she was stylishly dressed. Today's ensemble was a modern A-frame skirt in midnight hues, which ended above the knee, a simple black top, dangly earrings, and white hair pulled back in a loose bun. It was an outfit Connor's stylist might have picked out for me, except Etta wore it better. But under the clothes, makeup, and cocky attitude, her frame was bony and frail and her blue eyes watery. I felt a throb of dismay. Was it her health?

I knew she was old of course—in her seventies—but she made it so easy to forget the fact. She was ever elegant, smart as a whip, and had a zest for life that bordered on the wicked. I couldn't imagine her dear self drained of that vitality. Couldn't imagine the tedium of my apartment building without her.

I sat down.

She set her shoulders and pinned me with her gaze, nothing weak about it. "I know what you really do for a living."

My body froze while my mind raced. Over my oath of silence. The files I'd carefully hidden or destroyed. The lies I'd had to tell her, my housemate, my family, and now Connor's family too. How had she figured it out?

"I do understand why you've had to lie." She helped herself to a cookie from the plastic container I'd left on the table. "I'm not even angry about it. But there's no point going to such lengths to hide it from me now that I know."

My heart thudded along like a talentless three-year-old playing the bongo drum. Would they fire me? Or would they do worse than that? If there was one thing the Taste Society took seriously, it was secrecy. A Google search wouldn't reveal a scrap of genuine information about them. How was that possible in this day and age? Especially with the number of people who knew of their existence. How they contained the leaks was something I'd avoided thinking about too closely.

"They can't be mad at you for it," Etta said like she'd been reading my mind.

Maybe that's how she'd figured it out. Maybe she can read minds.

I shook my head, hoping to knock the silliness out of it.

If Etta could read minds, she was careful not to show amusement or alarm at my thoughts now. I remembered how, when I'd first met Etta, I'd suspected her of being a spy. Perhaps I should've listened to those instincts, as far out as they were . . .

"They don't need to find out that I know," she continued. "Same with your clients. Those highfalutin folks are awful precious about their privacy, but my knowing won't do them any harm. It'll be our secret. No need to look so anxious."

I forced a nod. "Okay. Thanks." My shoulders felt stiff—like the poop I was up to my neck in had caked and dried. "How . . . how did you figure it out?"

She finished off the rest of her cookie before answering. "I thought you'd never ask. It was simple—or should I say, elementary, my dear Watson. Get it?" She flashed a smile. "When I found out that you and Connor worked together, I looked him up and saw he was in private investigation and security. Since he was so rich, I figured he must have been working for rich people, and that made the whole classified angle make sense too, seeing as they can be snooty about that sort of thing. Anyway, because you have no discernible skills or qualifications in investigation and security—I mean, for Pete's sake, you don't even like guns—there was only one job description that made sense. You're a honeytrap!"

My mind boggled. She thought I was like one of those women in James Bond?

"That explains your widely varying wardrobe too. One day you're in clothes that have never been in fashion, the next you're the height of chic. At first I figured you wouldn't be any good at that either. No offense, you're cute and all, but you're not exactly a smooth seductress. But then I realized that's probably why you're so good at it. You're so naive and genuine that they'd never suspect a thing." She slapped her leg and cackled as if this was the best joke she'd ever heard.

I cracked my own smile, fighting like hell to keep my warring emotions off my face. Relief. Horror. Amusement. Fear at this new lie I'd have to embrace. "Very clever," I said. "You should've been an investigator yourself."

"Funny you should say that." Her eyes pinned me again. "That's why I'm telling you this. Because we have a case to solve."

3

I WAS AFRAID TO ASK. "A case?"

"Yes. Abe's been arrested."

She was talking about Abraham Black, the hired muscle who'd once tried to break my bones. He worked for the debt collection agency my loan shark back in Australia had enlisted to punish me when I was behind on my payments. Etta had since adopted him as a friend, mostly because she thought he was sexy.

My feelings for him were in a different category altogether. "What was he arrested for?"

"Murder."

"Shit, Etta. He's a bruiser. He probably did it."

"That's the same dumb-ass attitude that the police have. Just because his DNA's on the guy who went and became a root inspector—"

"Wait, became a what?"

"You know, the victim. He's checking out the grass from the other side. Taking a dirt nap. Going into the fertilizer business. Cashing in his chips. Basting the formaldehyde turkey—"

I held up a hand even though a morbid part of me wondered how long she could go on. "Got it."

"So we need to help clear Abe's name."

I still found her casual use of his first name weird. "Hang on a minute, why should we get involved? Let the police and the justice system do their work."

"I already told you. They've got the wrong attitude. It's an open-and-shut case as far as they're concerned."

"Maybe because it is."

She shot me a worse glare than the one she'd pulled out when I tried to give her a lesson on gun safety. It was true I wasn't a big fan of firearms, but I was a fan of safety. Etta was more casual about such things.

"Abe didn't do it, Isobel."

Oh boy, here came another lecture.

"Haven't you heard of innocent until proven guilty? You should be ashamed of yourself."

And I was, a bit, since she put it that way. When Mr. Black wasn't trying to break my bones, he seemed like a nice enough bloke.

"Okay, say he didn't do it, what makes you think we can prove that? Didn't you just finish telling me that I had no discernible skills in investigation work?"

"Well sure. But you must've picked up some tricks working as a honeytrap, right?"

I studied her face. Etta was a thrill seeker. In dangerous situations, she was in her element, whereas I was focusing on controlling my bladder. At present, there was too much excitement in her expression for comfort. But there was also a lot of righteous indignation and concern for her friend.

"I'll think about it," I told her. "But now I really need to get ready for work."

———

"ABSOLUTELY NOT," Connor said when I phoned and filled him in on Etta's proposal. I was driving to Vanessa Madison's house because she'd wanted to make sure I scrubbed up well enough to pass muster before my first public appearance. That and she needed to give me final instructions.

I overtook the car in front of me. If I got green lights and minimal traffic all the way, I might not be late. "That's what I thought you'd think, but Etta's a hard woman to say no to."

"Say it anyway."

I snorted. "Sure, I remember when you stayed in the car so you didn't have to face her wrath. And you don't live next door to her."

He let silence trickle down the line while I overtook another car.

I whooshed out a breath. "I'll think about it."

Connor remained quiet. He was master of using the power of silence to get people to talk, or in this case, concede.

Instead of conceding, I changed the subject. "So what are you up to tonight while I'm rubbing shoulders with some of LA's most privileged women? Don't you dare say it's classified."

"I'm having a quiet night in."

"Really?"

"You told me not to tell you it's classified."

Ugh. "Right. Well, I'm pulling into the driveway, so I've gotta go. Enjoy your quiet night."

Before I left the car, I reviewed my mental notes on the brief the Taste Society had given me. It was an unusually short Shade assignment. Since threats to someone's life or career were rarely fast to resolve, most lasted months and sometimes even years. But Vanessa Madison only required me for seven days.

The WECS Club prided themselves on their charitable donations, but their most renowned annual fundraiser was "A Scandalous Cause." It was a calendar that featured "tasteful, artistic, sensual" photos of the women from the club. For charity, naturally. Each beautiful, buffed, and surgically enhanced woman was posed and shot by fashion photographer Richard Newton, and the resulting photos were whittled down to the top twelve by superstar fashion designer René Laurent.

Hard to tell whether the good they did for each year's chosen charity outweighed the harm they did to women's rights.

The photo shoot was scheduled on January first, just a week away, and that was why Mrs. Madison had enlisted my services now. It was the biggest ego fest I'd ever heard of, and the winners would have a full twelve months to lord it over the losers.

Of course, the original photo shoot had been scheduled a month ago, leaving plenty of time for the calendar to be produced and delivered for the new year. But it seemed one of the women's sabotage attempts had gone awry. On the day of the shoot, the fashion photographer must have eaten something intended for one of the contestants and had been taken out of action by a dreadful case of diarrhea. Because he was in such high demand, the earliest he could reschedule was New Year's Day. Which was why the claws had come out yet again and why Vanessa had hired a Shade. It was up to me to ensure not a pimple or rash marred her skin, that her body didn't retain water, and that her digestive system stayed in excellent health.

The Madisons' maid let me in and showed me to a living area that was decorated similarly to the parlor but on a larger scale. Vanessa and a slender, dark-haired teenager who must be her daughter were sitting on the two lounges farthest apart. Vanessa with her spine straight and ankles crossed, and her daughter leaning against an armrest with her legs stretched out over the pale cream upholstery.

Vanessa beckoned, and I went to her like a well-trained dog. Her daughter might have paid more attention if I actually was a dog. She didn't bother to look up from her phone when we were introduced.

Wonderful to see an inflated sense of self-importance runs in the family.

I was wearing a floaty, mid-length beige skirt with matching three-inch heels and a white blouse. It was over the top and ill-suited for what was essentially a waitress role, but I'd wanted to please my new client.

Good dog.

Vanessa was dressed to intimidate in a deep red evening gown, red lipstick, and hair pinned into an elaborate updo. She practically oozed power, and I wondered what kind of man would choose her. Someone equally powerful? Or someone wanting to be led?

"What does Mr. Madison do?" I asked since no one else was talking.

The daughter snorted. "Anything with tits." Then she flounced off, perhaps before her mother could yell at her.

Vanessa, however, was unperturbed. "I send her to be educated at the prestigious Frederick Academy, and that's how she ends up speaking," she said dryly. "Whatever they're teaching her there, it's not manners." She gave a slight shake of her head—just enough to make her red hair catch the light. "My husband's a stockbroker. And we have an open marriage. He merely tends to take more advantage of it than I do."

Well, that was more information than I'd bargained for. She was so calm about it, as if it didn't bother her in the least. I almost believed she didn't. But there was a hint of tension around her mouth that made me remember she was a master of politics and power.

The game said if you couldn't control someone, you made it look like they were doing what you wanted anyway. If that wasn't possible, you could circumvent any power they'd won by convincing the other players that their actions had no impact on you. It seemed a lonely way to live.

Somehow I didn't think Vanessa would appreciate my sympathy.

She gestured for me to sit. "Now that my daughter

has kindly gone out of earshot, let me run over tonight with you."

───────────

IF THE WESTSIDE Elite Charity Social (WECS) Club was a nest of vipers, then my client was the Queen. Beautiful women orbited around her in clouds of swirling perfume and swishing fabric like she was the center of their universe. Even those that resisted the pull found their eyes slanting in her direction, monitoring, waiting, scheming.

The exclusive clubhouse was a graceful colonial building in Brentwood that overlooked lush, manicured gardens with an overabundance of rose bushes. Utterly impractical for the Los Angeles environment. The entire top floor had been turned into a single ballroom that served as a social and dining area, while downstairs boasted a full range of leisure and fitness offerings, from beauticians and masseuses to a gym with a pool. Tonight's get-together was on the top floor.

"I'll ignore you," Vanessa had warned me, "so that they'll ignore you. It's nothing personal." While the decision was strategic, we both knew she'd prefer to ignore me under normal circumstances as well. "Once they've dismissed you as beneath their notice, you can listen in on their conversations and tell me things I need to know."

"That's not part of my job description," I'd protested.

She'd counted out five one hundred dollar bills and slid them across the table. "It is for an extra grand. You'll get the rest on January first when you've proven yourself."

I'd bitten my tongue and taken the money.

Now I stood on the outskirts, my back to the wall, waiting to be summoned like a condemned poison taster for an ancient king. She had a glass of wine in her hand but never sipped it.

True to her word, I was, for all intents and purposes, invisible.

I was also trying not to breathe. Expensive fragrance coated the air. Alluring, exotic, fresh, or playful, it didn't matter. Each of them affected my abilities to taste and smell clearly.

We'd done a whole course on this during my Shade training. There were three issues at work: olfactory fatigue which reduced your overall sense of smell and was caused by smelling new scent after new scent; olfactory habituation, whereafter being exposed to the same scent for a length of time, the body temporarily filters it out so you can't smell that particular scent; and olfactory irritation or distraction, where your sense of smell is temporarily impaired by strong or irritable scents.

Experts were uncertain whether these impairments were caused physiologically by the scents coating the olfactory receptors or psychologically through the brain's processing of information from those receptors. To combat this, we'd spent months smelling every base note commonly found in relevant poisons, learning them intimately and visualizing them to make it easier for us to register and identify them in unideal situations.

I was listening to a heated debate over the merits of Botox versus Dysport when Vanessa beckoned me forward. Did these women know that both of those drugs had been developed from the same bacterium that caused life-threatening botulism?

"I'm hungry," Vanessa said. "Find me something to eat."

"Yes, Mrs. Madison."

She'd made arrangements with the kitchen staff. I was her spiritual food adviser, whatever the heck that was, and would oversee her meals myself to ensure they matched her aura. In reality, I would go to the kitchen, choose a meal option I could taste without ruining the presentation of the food, then serve her myself and watch like a hawk to make sure no one slipped anything into it after I'd already tested it. My eyes felt tired already.

I wound my way through the clusters of women, hoping to overhear something that would be of interest to Vanessa. Almost everyone was talking about their beauty preparations for the calendar photo shoot, except one pair boasting about their cherubs' achievements at the

Frederick Academy and another who said something about a gun. The last made me pause, but their voices were hushed and I couldn't pick up any more without being obvious about it.

Before entering the bustle of the downstairs kitchen, I stepped outside for a moment and dragged in lungfuls of clean air. It was nearing dusk, but the rose gardens were artfully illuminated by night lights. I admired the sight while breathing deeply to refresh my mind and sense of smell before performing the tasting. For good measure, I buried my nose in the crook of my arm. It was a technique professional perfumers used to bring their olfactory sense back to its normal baseline, and one of the reasons Shades used low-scented beauty products.

In the kitchen, today's appetizers were soft-shell crab, heirloom tomato and pancetta ravioli, beet, walnut, and goat's feta salad, or a seafood velouté. I opted for the velouté, which from what I could see was just a fancy word for white sauce, because it would be possible to taste without leaving obvious marks on the presentation. That and I didn't feel like salad.

I tasted the velouté carefully. The scallops, shrimp, and oysters were fresh and tender, and the white sauce was the perfect blend of creamy, salty, and tart. It crossed my mind that if Connor and I didn't work out, I should see if the chef was single.

I dismissed the idea seconds later of course. While I had, on occasion, allowed my stomach to overrule my brain, I liked to think I was smart enough not to let it dictate my love life.

In addition to the obvious ingredients, I could taste lemon juice, dry vermouth, fish sauce, and at least four different fresh herbs. I wanted to eat more, but I'd already established it was clear of poisons.

As I carried it up the stairs and navigated my way through the women milling around the ballroom, I was grateful my years as a barista had prepared me for the challenge. Until a jostle to the back of my elbow sent a wave of that delicious velouté slopping down my shirtfront.

"Isobel Avery, is that you?" said a voice that was unpleasantly familiar. "What a shame. You seem to have spilled something."

I turned slowly to delay the moment of our reacquaintance for a few meager seconds. "What are you doing here?"

Emily Lin flicked her long black hair away from her lovely oval face and eyed my chest where the warm, creamy fish sauce was seeping through to my skin. "Same as you, I'd bet. Only I'm doing a better job."

Yep, that was the Emily I knew and disliked. She'd gone through Shade training with me, and the two of us had been top of the class. Instead of bringing us together, it had turned her into the closest thing I'd ever had to an arch nemesis. Ultra-competitive, she'd been determined to beat me at every test, and she wasn't afraid to play dirty to do it.

"That must be why the Taste Society chose me to protect the WECS Club president, Vanessa Madison," I said. "Who are you here for?"

A frown marred Emily's forehead, confirming my hope she was working for a lower-ranking client.

"Anyway," I continued. "I'd better be off. You know how the Taste Society doesn't like fraternizing among Shades." I pushed past her and retreated down the stairs.

4

MY FEET WERE KILLING ME by the time I got
home. Why I had to dress up and wear heels when
I was supposed to be invisible anyway was beyond my
understanding.

I'd cleaned my shirt as best as I could under the circumstances and then borrowed an apron from the waitstaff to
cover the mess, but I could still smell the seafood velouté.
And while it had been delicious to eat, no one wants to
smell like a fish market.

I stripped the offending garment off only to find that
the scent had soaked into my skin like a nasty perfume.
Great. Looks like I'd need to have yet another shower today.
I'd have to go to a pharmacy and get eye drops as well. I'd
never stared, too worried to blink, for so long in my life.

I was grateful that my housemate Oliver was away in England. He was good company, but sometimes nothing beat being alone. Well, alone with a cat, I amended when Meow wound her lithe, tiger-striped body around my ankles. She'd probably been drawn by the fishy odor. I picked her up and hugged her to my chest anyway. "You and I are going to have the best night tonight. I'll get you some food, jump in the shower, and then it's you, me, bed, and a book, what do you say?" She head-butted my chin in agreement.

When I felt the rasp of her tongue on my seafood-scented skin, I put her down and rummaged for the can opener. Someone knocked on the door.

Damn. I threw the stinky blouse back over my head and answered it.

"Finally you're home," Etta said. "You need to come with me."

"I need to go to bed," I corrected.

She put a hand on one hip and gave me the devil eye. "Oh, you'd like that, wouldn't you? Poor Abe is curled up in some jail cell while his wife and daughter are crying themselves to sleep with worry, and you need to go to bed. I don't think so. Not until you've looked his daughter in the eye and explained to her why you won't be helping bring her daddy home."

I rolled my eyes up to the ceiling. Ugh, I needed to get

a broom out to get rid of those cobwebs. "This is blackmail you know."

She grabbed my arm and pulled me toward the door. "I know."

I wasn't a complete pushover. I fed Meow first.

Sitting in the passenger seat of Etta's 1970s, buttercup-yellow Dodge Charger, I closed my eyes. In part because they were so tired, and in part because her driving made me nervous.

"Now, Izzy, Mr. Black's wife and daughter are . . . special. I need you to be on your best behavior."

My eyelids sprang open. I'd never received a warning to behave from Etta. Of the pair of us, she was far more likely to act badly, and almost every conversation we had included her telling me to let loose, get a greater sense of adventure, and live a little.

"No matter how you feel about Abe, you need to keep it to yourself," she continued. "To these two, he's their adored, loving father and husband. And you better keep the lid on it tight. Joy, that's his daughter, is a real smart cookie. Real smart. You know she earned herself a scholarship to the swanky Frederick Academy? She'll pick up on any hints you drop."

Wasn't that where Vanessa's daughter went? If so, the scholarship must've been worth thousands. I felt chastened and hoped I could hide my feelings adequately. "Got it."

We drove in silence for a few minutes before Etta broke it again. "I don't know why you hold such a grudge anyway. Abe never actually hurt you."

Only because I ran away as fast as I could. And then made a bargain with him through a window with a Taser between us.

Okay, he'd been apologetic about it, and most bruisers probably wouldn't have struck a bargain with me, let alone honored it. But it's hard to think well of someone after the terror of being chased down the street, certain you're about to have your bones broken one by one. I'd always disliked jogging, but now I was scarred for life, so it would be his fault if I got fat too.

Even pushing my feelings about Mr. Black aside, this whole thing reeked of being a bad idea. It was one thing to assist Connor—a professional investigator who had agreements with the police—to investigate a case. Especially one I had personal involvement in. But it was quite another to work without any professional guidance or approval and paired with an amateur septuagenarian sleuth who was entirely too fond of adventure and her Glock.

I shuddered to imagine what Police Commander Hunt would have to say about it should he find out. He'd put me in handcuffs for interference quicker than Meow could catch a cockroach. Not that there was any reason for him to find out, but still. And if Mr. Black didn't murder the victim, then someone else did. Someone who wouldn't appreciate us poking around. Someone who had a track record of murdering people they didn't appreciate.

Connor was right. "Absolutely not" should be my answer. I spent the rest of the trip steeling myself to stay strong no matter what Etta had planned for me.

———

MR. BLACK'S HOME WAS, to put it nicely, a pile of crap. It was a small, squat building in Vermont Square that needed a new roof, a new fence, and a new coat of paint. A beat-up, maroon Dodge minivan from a former century sat out front.

Contrary to Etta's prediction, Mr. Black's wife and daughter were not crying in their beds, but they both had anxiety pinching their faces despite their efforts to hide it. Mrs. Black, or Hallie as she'd asked me to call her, was in a wheelchair, and their thirteen-year-old daughter Joy had a black eye and a bandaged wrist. For a brief second I wondered whether it was for show to garner my sympathy. Then I shoved the notion away, ashamed to have thought it. As if my scanty detective skills were worth the effort.

"Hallie and I will put the kettle on," Etta said. "Why don't you let Joy show you what she's been working at?"

Joy gave me a shy smile. "Did you wanna see?" She was small and skinny and seemed to be made up of all arms and legs. The exact opposite of her father. She wore her hair in a tight braid that was too severe for her thin face and large brown eyes. Although now at the end of a long day, some less cooperative tendrils had slipped free.

"I'd love to," I said.

It was impossible not to appreciate the differences between Vanessa's daughter and Joy. I hoped the posh school wouldn't tarnish her sweetness.

She led me out to the backyard and switched on the outdoor lights. There appeared to be some sort of obstacle course set up on the dried-out lawn. There were a bunch of solid-looking platforms of varying sizes and angles made from packing crates, a sturdy picnic bench, several bars including an old swing set without a swing, and a ten-foot section of wall mounted to a tree.

"Watch this." Joy peeled off her faded purple jacket and sprinted at the first bar which she leaped up and grabbed, then swung, twisted, and launched herself onto a nearby platform like an acrobat. Except instead of sticking the landing and taking a bow, she rolled with the momentum and leaped onto the next platform, then threw herself at the wall, which she managed to run up in defiance of gravity. She used the wall to change direction and then ran in a series of precise leaps from the picnic bench to several of the platforms, followed by a bar that I would've slipped off even without her speed, and finished with another acrobatic flip.

I clapped as she landed and jogged over to me, her face flushed.

"It's called parkour," she explained. "It might seem crazy, but there's real strategy and technique and discipline involved—like a non-combative martial art. I love it!"

"Is that how you hurt your wrist?"

"Uh, yeah. Normally I'd do more swings and stuff, except I'm meant to be resting the sprain. But it's not that dangerous if you don't do it on rooftops and that kinda thing. Mom and Dad let me practice since it's the one type of physical exercise I'm interested in. It challenges my mind and my body at the same time, and I don't like team sports or anything. Well, I'm pretty sure. I'm not that popular at school, so I wouldn't get picked anyway." The last admission had her gaze dropping to the ground, her scuffed-up sneaker playing in the dirt.

"Well I'm impressed," I said. "What did you say it was called?"

Her eyes lit up again. "Parkour! Did you know it was developed from military obstacle course training?"

After Joy finished enlightening me about this whole new world of exercise, we returned to the kitchen for the promised cups of tea.

"He hates that job," Hallie told me when we'd all settled around the dining table. Like her kitchen, she was small and neat, used to making the most of what she'd been given. And she believed her husband would never have been arrested if it wasn't for his profession as a bruiser. "You know the first time he had to hurt someone, he came home and cried?"

I felt a stab of disbelief. "Then why does he do it?"

Her voice cracked. "For us. He does it for his family. He got laid off from his factory job at General Motors three years ago and couldn't find another position. He applied for anything and everything, but twelve months passed, and we couldn't remortgage the house anymore. We sold it, moved here, and still couldn't put food on the table. When the debt collectors came knocking, they made a comment about taking Joy as collateral, and he threw them out on their asses and sent them running home with their tails between their legs. Their boss offered him the job."

"Mom, swear jar." Joy pushed a battered porcelain pig onto the table using her one good hand. The parkour demonstration must have taken a toll on her injured wrist.

Hallie tearfully pulled a coin out of her pocket and popped it in. "Sorry, honey."

Joy patted her mom's shoulder. "It's okay. It'll be okay.

They'll get him out of this, won't you?"

She turned her wide eyes to me, and I had the distinct impression she'd figured out what was going on and was playing me like a fool. Nevertheless, it worked.

"All right. Tell me about the case."

It was Joy who answered. "Dad was just in the wrong place at the wrong time. Mr. Bergström, that's his boss, told him to go beat the victim up. So he did. The coroner placed the time of death about an hour later. A nosy old man across the road saw Dad leaving, so there's an eyewitness and his DNA on the vic. But it doesn't prove he did it. They don't have a motive or a murder weapon. It's all circumstantial. And Dad would never kill someone. He doesn't enjoy hurting people, but the police like him for it anyway. They're prejudiced because of his job, but that's wrong. That's not what the law says. But humans are imperfect, so we need to accept it and then convince them otherwise."

I heard my teeth click together as I shut my gaping jaw.

"You must think I'm crazy to let my daughter know all this," Hallie said, wiping her eyes again. "But when she's determined, I can't stop her from finding anything out, and I'd prefer she learned it in openness and safety rather than whatever nefarious means she'd cook up otherwise." She sent a fond, weary look at Joy.

Joy's eyes were still fastened on me.

Fool that I am, I found myself saying, "We can't promise anything, but we'll do what we can to make sure the right person goes to prison for this."

My last thought as my head hit the pillow was how I was going to break the news to Connor.

5

IT TURNED OUT that I didn't have to work out how to tell Connor. At least not straight away. He texted me to say he wouldn't be able to make our afternoon date.

I was disappointed, but it was the nature of our jobs. Both of us were essentially on call twenty-four hours a day, seven days a week, which was why the last two days—Christmas, which we'd spent with his family, and our lazy afternoon yesterday—had been so special. Even if they did involve a poisoning, an intimidating new client, and a lack of any real conversation.

I booted up Oliver's laptop with my morning cup of tea and Googled the murder victim's name. Michael Watts was the CEO of a lucrative wholesale distribution company that sold sporting equipment to retailers all over the country. The company had been founded by Michael's grandfather and then passed down the family line until Michael was in charge.

A deeper search revealed that two warehouses had shut down in the last year, suggesting that it wasn't going so well. Maybe that's how he'd racked up enough debt for someone to send Mr. Black after him. He could be living beyond his means to avoid public humiliation or acquiring cash off the books to buoy up the company. But who had lent him the money? And why would they hire a bruiser to scare him into repaying the debt only to kill him an hour later?

His corporate profile showed a handsome, athletic-looking man with a bleached-white smile. He'd won a local golf tournament last year, and his name also came up alongside various sport-related donations or sponsorships.

I went to his Facebook page next. His privacy settings didn't allow me to see much, but there was a photo of him, arm slung around a dainty brunette, and a teenager I assumed was their son. A few minutes later, I'd managed to find both of their profiles too. His wife, Nicole Watts, was a member of the WECS Club, and his son, also named Michael, went to the Frederick Academy like every other WECS Club member's child I'd heard about. I guessed that the club either recruited most of its members from mothers at the Frederick Academy, or its members were so competitive that sending their children to one of the most expensive schools in America was par for the course.

Out of interest, I looked up the annual tuition. Then I wished I hadn't. It was forty grand a year. Per child.

That was even more concerning when I converted it to Australian dollars.

If I was lucky, the links between the WECS Club and Frederick Academy could work in my favor. Maybe I'd overhear some useful gossip while eavesdropping for Vanessa. Or maybe the WECS Club women were so self-absorbed that the murder of someone they knew would garner only fleeting attention in the lead up to the Scandalous Cause calendar.

The news coverage of Michael Watts's death didn't say much beyond he'd been found shot in his home Christmas Eve and that police were investigating. I wondered which unfortunate detective had gotten the Christmas shift. There was another article from last night mentioning that they had a suspect in custody. It named the suspect as Abraham Black, but there were no helpful details illuminating why the police believed he'd done it and whether they'd explored any other avenues.

Amateur sleuths in stories always had chatty contacts at the local police station, but the one policeman I knew personally was Police Commander Hunt—the top-secret LAPD liaison assigned to the Taste Society. After working with him on the last case, I was pretty sure he'd prefer to shoot me rather than help me. He'd certainly throw my ass in jail if he found out I was interfering with one of his cases. I knew because he'd done it before.

The last thing I looked up was Michael's obituary. It was the run-of-the-mill line about how he was a loving father and husband who was survived by his wife and son that got to me. Such an ordinary line, but after the death of my client less than two weeks ago and seeing the devastation it caused his mom and best friend, I knew how much grief that short statement hid behind it.

I didn't let myself think about what it would mean if Mr. Black really was responsible for this man's death. Instead, I sifted through the usual motives. Money. Power. Love or sex. Or secrets.

It didn't help. Michael Watts had power and money (albeit perhaps less of it than he was used to), he had a wife, which meant the love and sex motives were on the table, and he could have stumbled across a big secret. Any of them could apply.

The one positive was that none of them seemed to fit Mr. Black. But if he wasn't guilty—a point I was unconvinced on—how the heck were we going to find out who was?

As far as I could see, we had two avenues for rustling up other potential suspects. One was to learn more about the victim. That would be challenging since there was no way I was about to question his grieving widow and the wealthy crowd wasn't going to talk when we didn't even have a PI license for credibility. The other was to find out who else the police had looked into. That would also be tricky with a sad lack of any handy-dandy contacts.

I closed the laptop. Mr. Black's arraignment hearing was scheduled late this morning, so maybe he'd be able to tell us more after he'd been released on bail. Until then, I'd have to explain to Etta that we were at a dead end.

———————

"DEAD END? What nonsense. Didn't you hear Joy mention a neighbor who saw Abe leaving the Watts' residence around the time of the murder?"

"Sure, but we don't know which neighbor, and why would they talk to us?"

Etta shook her head. "Have you never read a cozy mystery? There's a nosy neighbor on every street, and I'm willing to bet that it was them who was the witness. Michael was shot in the middle of the day. Who else has time to peer out their window and take note of strangers coming and going on the day before Christmas for goodness' sake? A nosy person, that's who. And the thing about nosy people is that they're bored, and they're bored because they're lonely. And you know what lonely people like? Someone to talk to."

I wondered if Etta was such an expert on this because she was in part describing herself. She knew everything that happened in our apartment building, she often complained about being bored, and she certainly liked to talk. Yet she was so smart and self-assured that I'd never thought of her as lonely before.

I didn't let my thoughts show. "But how would we find this person?"

"Easy. They needed a line of sight to the house, so that'll narrow it down to a couple of neighbors. Most people should either be at work or out and about enjoying their holidays, but the lonely soul is probably home alone. So we'll knock on doors and ask."

I had to admit, it was a clever plan, as long as her assumptions held up. "But how do we get the victim's address without speaking to Mr. Black?"

She looked at me like I was an idiot. "We have his full name, his wife's name, and the suburb he lives in from the news articles. Haven't you ever heard of a phone book? It's even easier these days with it being online. Now stop coming up with excuses and let's get going."

I knew there was no way she'd let it go until we'd at

least tried. "Okay. I have a couple of hours until I need to go to work."

"We'll take my car. It's spiffier than yours. But bring some cookies. I've been too wound up and excited to eat breakfast."

Half an hour later, we were out the front of the Watts' residence in Pacific Palisades. It was a dark brick two-story building with bright white eaves, window frames, and accents. A matching white balcony supported by ornate columns sat above the front entrance. The homes here rivaled Connor's in size, and those on the Watts' side of the street backed onto the Riviera Country Club golf course for beautiful views.

Of course, we were only interested in those that had views to the Watts' estate. Thick hedges between the adjoining properties blocked the ground floor line of sight, but since the homes were all two-story, it was possible the nosy neighbor we were looking for could live in either of the houses directly next door or one of two properties across the street. A fifth property would have had a view if it weren't for a giant, evergreen ash tree.

Between the trees lining the road, the verdant, manicured gardens, and the beautiful homes, it was a pretty street. Hard to imagine Mr. Black driving here in his worn-out, wheelchair-accessible minivan and killing one of the residents.

We ruled out two of the houses when nobody came to the door. The lonely neighbor we were looking for shouldn't have anywhere else to be. A third we dismissed because the surplus of cars in the driveway suggested they had guests over. Not because these homeowners couldn't afford a surplus of cars themselves, but because they could also afford to keep them garaged.

We tried the estate directly across from the Watts' place, and an elderly gentleman in a monogrammed maroon bathrobe answered. "Well, aren't you two a sight for old eyes," he said when he sighted us on the porch. Those "old eyes" were bloodshot with a web of veins that matched his bathrobe. "Who did I impress to deserve you knocking on my door?"

Etta shot me an "I told you so" look before laying on the charm. "Why I can tell you're deserving just by looking at you. We were wondering if you might be able to help us with an important investigation. About the murder that happened across the road."

"You don't look like police."

Etta laughed. "We aren't! And I'm sure thankful about that. We're looking into it for a concerned friend of ours."

The man's shoulders sagged, causing the bathrobe to gape wider at his chest and confirm my misgiving that he had nothing on underneath.

"Oh, is this a special friend of yours?"

Etta gave a playful push to his drooping shoulder. "No, not that kind. I'm as free as the day I was born. Why do you ask, you old devil?"

"Because I was thinking of inviting you on a date later."

"I'll look forward to your invitation then," Etta said, letting herself inside, "after you've helped us with a few questions we have."

I followed her, and we settled in a room with an abundance of chandeliers, gold, and expensive antique furniture. The chandeliers didn't cast enough light to offset the dark wallpaper and furnishings, and the air smelled of dust and stale cigar smoke. Etta seated herself beside our nosy neighbor while I chose a spot facing them.

"What did you want to know?" the man asked. He sat with his legs wide, and I was grateful his robe was of sufficient length for that not to matter.

Etta leaned toward him. "What is the Watts family like?"

"Normal by the standards of people around here I suppose. A bit noisy occasionally, with yelling or music, but that's what happens when you've got a teenager in the house. Can't be helped. Believe it or not, I was a naughty teenager once."

He waggled his eyebrows at the word naughty.

"You don't need to convince me," Etta said. "I still like to be naughty sometimes."

I wondered if either of them would notice if I hid behind the settee I was sitting on and stuck my fingers in my ears.

"Did the police talk to you about the murder?" Etta all but stage whispered the word "murder"—like someone who thought it was fun scandalous gossip rather than a tragedy. I wasn't sure if that bit was an act or not.

"Yes. I was very helpful because I saw somebody leave the house within the hours they thought it had happened."

"Is that the one they arrested?"

He nodded, pride as plain on his face as his overly long nostril hair.

"Did they ask you anything else?"

"Sure, loads of questions."

"Like what? What did you tell them?"

"Like whether I'd seen anything odd lately, so I told them about this crazy cat video I came across on the Google, and then they said they meant anything odd happening on this street or around the Watts' house. So I told them about a lady I noticed watching the house about a week back. She didn't get out of the car, and she left after Mr. Watts did. I wrote down her license plate because I know that's what you're supposed to do when you see something suspicious."

"Where is it?"

"The license number? I gave it to the police."

Damn. He might as well have tossed it in a piranha tank for all the good it'd do us there.

"Can you describe the lady in the car?" Etta asked.

"Let's see . . . White. Young and pretty. Brown hair. Wearing those giant sunglasses that are the fashion these days. I don't know why everyone likes them so much when they remind me of oversized bug eyes."

"How young?"

"In her thirties or forties? I'm not sure. Everyone seems young when you get to my age. Not that I've forgotten how to act young if you get my drift. That's what counts."

"Young at heart. Absolutely. Do you remember what sort of car it was?"

"A dark blue Honda Civic."

One of the most popular cars in LA.

Etta got to her feet and fluffed her hair flirtatiously. "Well, sir, you've been mighty helpful to some ladies in need. You give me a call sometime about that date."

He stood there, beaming ear-to-ear as we made our exit, never realizing that she hadn't given him her number.

6

"THAT WAS KIND OF MEAN," I told her. "What's wrong with him? Why not let him take you on a date?" Etta seemed to be on a date every other night. How hard could it be to add one more to her rotation? After her explanation about his loneliness, I felt bad for the guy.

He'd have to get rid of the nostril hair though.

Etta flapped a hand at me. "Are you kidding? He's way too old."

By that, she meant he was close to her own age. I knew better than to argue, so I checked the time instead. "Let's go pick up Mr. Black."

We'd offered to drive him home after his arraignment and bail hearing since his car was at the house where they'd arrested him and Hallie couldn't drive.

He looked exhausted. An overnight stay in jail would do that to you, as I'd found out from experience. But somehow I'd expected a man who looked like the Hulk would fare better than me.

We stopped at a diner so Mr. Black could eat something more satisfying than jail rations and we could talk to him without his family having to go over it all again.

"It was a professional job," he told us after wolfing down a stack of pancakes. "My boss, Mr. Bergström, instructed me to go and rough him up a little, so that's what I did." He wiped a giant hand over his face and rubbed his clean-shaven scalp. "He was alive when I left. I've never killed nobody."

His gentle brown eyes—the same as Joy's—were soft, pleading, and I felt myself beginning to believe him.

"Then you didn't know him personally?" I asked. "His kid goes to the same school as Joy."

He rubbed his skull again. "There was nothing personal about it."

"Then why are the police so sure it was you? While your profession isn't exactly . . . legal, it gives you a reason to be there, and there's no motive for murder from a debt-collection perspective."

"My boss is denying that he told me to go in the first place. Doesn't want the police looking into his books, I'm guessing."

"Hell." Etta's tone was so sharp I suspected she'd been thinking of a different word. "Doesn't he have any loyalty toward you?"

Mr. Black shrugged his massive shoulders. They were wide enough that Etta and I could have sat on one each, without even half a butt cheek hanging off the edge. "The old boss might've, but Mr. Bergström's new. Why stick his neck out?"

"Why indeed," Etta muttered, and I felt a twinge of foreboding she might be hatching up a plan to change Mr. Bergström's mind.

"Do you know anything about the victim?" I asked. "What information do you get for a job?"

"Just the name and a list of addresses they might be found at, sometimes a photo and details of their debt. But there weren't any photos or loan info for this one."

"Did you keep the addresses?"

"The officer who arrested me grabbed the list, but since I visited each location, I think I can remember them."

"Good." I dug a pen and scrap of paper out of my bag. "Can you write them down for us?"

His handwriting was surprisingly neat as he printed them out.

"And did you notice anything when you were at Michael Watts's house?" I asked. "Anything to suggest why someone else might want him dead? Or anyone else in the area?"

"Not that I can think of. I wasn't there that long, and I made sure there was no one around before I went in. Didn't want to upset his wife and kid. It was bad enough to beat him up on Christmas Eve."

He set the pen down and looked at Etta. Maybe he knew she was the more sympathetic party. "It's bad, isn't it? I don't think the police are even looking at other possibilities."

It took me a minute to recognize the expression on his face since I'd never have expected to see it there. Fear.

"Don't you worry, Abe." Etta patted his hand. Hers looked like a child's patting a grizzly bear paw. "Izzy and I will take care of it."

Mr. Black turned those brown eyes on me, and I tried not to show my doubts about that.

"Thank you. It really means a lot." He wiped moisture from his cheeks. "I can't leave Hallie and Joy. I can't."

———

WE DROPPED Mr. Black home, and even I got moisture in my eyes watching Joy run and Hallie wheel out to see him. The momentous weight of what we'd agreed to do sat heavy on my conscience.

Etta, on the other hand, was buoyant. "We'll talk to the police next," she said. "Find out whether it's true they're no longer investigating other possibilities and if they had any other suspects before deciding it was Abe."

"You're a civilian," I said, remembering Hunt sneering the word at me. "They're not going to just hand you their case files."

"You let me take care of that," she said.

She drove us home to pick up Dudley. We hadn't been able to take him with us this morning since he wouldn't fit in the car with Mr. Black. Heck, Mr. Black barely fit in Etta's car full stop. She shooed me over to my own apartment and told me to refresh myself with a cup of tea while she took care of something.

Ten minutes later, she opened the door with Dudley in tow. Dudley was a sleek black ex-racing greyhound she'd rescued as an early Christmas present to herself. Contrary to my preconceived ideas about the breed, he was the laziest dog I'd ever met and liked nothing more than a soft bed, paired with copious cuddles and treats. It was impossible to tell whether Dudley or Etta was more pleased with their new living companion.

I was almost as pleased as they were. I smooched Dudley on his long nose and showered him with pets before giving Etta my attention. When I did, I took an involuntary step back.

"What are you wearing?" I asked, shocked to see her looking like . . . well, a little old lady.

She tugged the shapeless knit cardigan that draped over her equally shapeless full-length skirt. A pair of sneakers I'd never seen before peeked out underneath. "Oh, this? It's my harmless-old-lady outfit." She grinned, and I noticed her lipstick was applied slightly off-center, with a pink smear on one tooth. "That reminds me, I need to grab my walking stick." Sure enough, she retrieved an ugly black walking stick with a quad-legged base for extra stability.

I was speechless.

She grinned again. "Wait until you see this baby in action."

We went in Etta's Charger again. She'd purchased a pet hammock that hung over the rear footwells to turn the narrow backseat area into a padded bed for Dudley. Because it was a two-door car, Dudley shared my window, his wet nose quivering by my ear for most of the trip. Lucky he didn't drool. Much, anyway.

We arrived at the 27th Street Community Police Station that was handling Mr. Black's case. The old two-story gray brick building stirred up bad memories since it was here that Hunt worked and where he'd thrown me in jail. But it was a big station and the chances of running into him were slim.

Both valid points, yet somehow the butterflies in my stomach weren't buying it.

It was a cool day, so we left Dudley in the car with the windows cracked. As always, he was quite content chilling on his hammock, though he'd prefer it if we stayed with him.

I would prefer that too.

"Maybe I should keep Dudley company while you go in without me," I said as Etta checked her skewed lipstick and put on a pair of coke-bottle glasses to complete her transformation.

"Get your ass out of that seat. You agreed to help me with this, and I'm gonna hold you to it."

I got out and followed her inside.

Etta shuffled up to the front desk, her walking stick thudding heavily against the dark tiles. I could almost see the policeman behind it soften at the picture she presented. "How can I help you, ma'am?"

She leaned in and put a hand on the counter as if to steady herself. "It's my grandson." Her voice wobbled like she was about to start crying. "I heard he's in some trouble, and I was hoping to speak to the detective in charge."

"Well, sure. I'll see if the detective is available. Otherwise, I'm sure we can find someone to talk to you. What's your grandson's name?"

"Oh, thank you. It's Abe. I mean Abraham.

"And last name?"

"Oops, sorry. My mental faculties ain't what they used to be. It's Black. Like the color."

"Great. You take a seat, and I'll find someone to talk to you. Help yourself to a drink of water from the dispenser over there too."

As soon as he left, Etta beamed at me. "See? Most people will fall over themselves to be kind when I'm in my harmless-old-lady outfit."

Across the room from us was an open-plan office area. We sat in the uncomfortable chairs and watched the officers in their uncomfortable chairs. It gave me even more respect for law enforcement. In addition to being out on the streets facing violence, hostility, and danger every day to keep us safe, they returned to their desks and had to deal with these torture devices.

Maybe someone up in headquarters had figured it would keep them eager to get into their vehicles—if only to stretch their aching backs and return circulation to their posteriors.

I was halfway through composing an imaginary letter of complaint to headquarters when an authoritative figure strode toward us.

"Cripes. Is that Police Commander Hunt?" Etta asked, getting to her feet.

I'd been thinking the exact same thing, except with a worse curse word.

"I can't let him see me like this!" Etta sounded well and truly panicked—the first time I'd ever witnessed such a thing. She had a crush on him.

"Better you than me," I said, jumping up and turning to flee. It was then I noticed she was already gone.

I used that word again, the one worse than cripes.

Hunt's eyes lasered in on me, and I knew it was too late to run, despite every instinct screaming at me to do so.

"You," he said.

The man in front of me would look equally at home facing down an irate bull with nothing more than a lasso or jumping out of a military aircraft on a covert ops mission. His face was sun weathered and lined, his buzz cut a steel gray, and despite having had a good sixty-five years to soften, he was all hard muscle under that uniform. Where he didn't fit in so well was with the LAPD's public relations push for their personnel to be more friendly and approachable.

I raised my hand in an awkward wave, squelching down my anxiety. "Did you have a nice Christmas?" I asked. Maybe he did. Maybe it'd put him in a better mood to think about it.

"Henderson told me a relative of our top suspect wanted to talk to someone about the Watts case. How're you and Abraham Black related?"

"Uh." No point in lying . . . on that issue. "We're not.

I guess Henderson got muddled up. I hear police work is pretty stressful and all. Maybe he should get some paid time off or some counseling."

Hunt stepped closer, and I shut my trap. "You're yammering, buying time to come up with a stupid story."

I shook my head, thinking fast to do exactly that. "No. I just wanted to make sure you'd checked it wasn't poison." After meeting the WECS Club women, I guess I had a whole new appreciation for how much the rich and powerful liked sabotaging each other. Plus it was the one excuse for my presence here that he might deem acceptable.

His mustache bristled like it was getting ready to launch from his face and attack me. So much for my acceptable theory.

"He was shot. In the head." He pointed to the center of his forehead, in case I didn't get it.

He'd told me a detail I didn't know. The papers had said Mr. Watts had been shot, but not in the head. That could be meaningful.

Hunt was expecting a response, so I stuck with my impromptu reason for being here. "But had he been drugged before that? Was he alive when the bullet went in?"

He sneered. "You know something I don't, Avery?"

"Um."

"You're talking garbage, and you're fishing. I'm going to give you the benefit of the doubt and assume you didn't know I was leading the case. Now you do."

He stepped another inch closer until I could smell what he'd had for breakfast—engine-grease coffee, beef jerky, and . . . was that marshmallow Pop-Tart?

"Stay the hell out of my investigation, you hear me?"

Using every ounce of will I possessed (and focusing on that whiff of marshmallow Pop-Tart), I managed not to step back. Rule number one when dealing with bullies: never show fear.

"Are you worried I'll make you look bad by solving the case again?" I asked sweetly.

His face mottled with red, and his mustache bristled further.

"Get. Out."

I gave him a perky salute to distract from my quaking knees. "Nice to see you, Commander."

———

"YOU ABANDONED ME!" I fumed when I found Etta leaning against the car, having a cigarette. "And I thought you were quitting."

She'd taken up smoking a year ago for no other reason than that it felt good. But now she had Dudley whom she wanted to protect from secondhand smoke, standing outside made the tobacco hit more trouble than it was worth. Unfortunately, she was finding that quitting the habit was harder than taking it up in the first place.

"That was stressful," she said. "Can you imagine if he saw me like this? I needed to calm my nerves."

I threw myself into my seat. I needed to calm my nerves too, so I reached for the cookies. The container was empty.

I thrust it out the window at her. "Seriously?"

She extinguished her cigarette and climbed in beside me. "You should've brought more if you wanted some. Why are you so worked up anyway?"

Her question reminded me that Etta didn't know my history with Hunt. She'd only met him once when he'd come to pick up a severed appendage that had been gifted to me. My annoyance faded. A bit.

"Well? Did you get any information out of him?"

"No. Except that Michael was shot in the head. I guess I need a harmless-old-lady outfit too."

"You just work on improving your honeytrap act, dear. Harmless old lady is what you've got me for." She started the engine. "Time for round two."

Mr. Bergström's office was a transportable building chocked up on cinder blocks next to a metal recycling place in Redondo Junction. It was far from glamorous, and I had an uneasy feeling his choice might have something to do with the convenient vicinity to those giant metal-crushing machines which could smash a human body into nice, hideable pieces.

Perhaps Etta had the same thought or saw the look on my face because she slipped her beloved Glock out of her bag and said, "Don't stress, I've got your back."

Dudley, who we'd brought with us out of the car this time, had no such qualms and was busy lifting a leg on one of those cinder blocks. I really hoped Mr. Bergström wasn't watching us through the window. Or on those surveillance cameras. Ugh.

Etta put her Glock away and tapped on the door. A slim man with slicked back blond hair opened it. There was something odd about him, and it took me a minute to realize it was because his eyebrows were so pale they were almost invisible. He arched one of them when he took in our ragtag group. "Ladies, are you sure you're in the right place?"

"Of course I'm sure, young man. I'm old but I'm not senile." As if remembering her outfit, Etta softened the words with a smile.

"All right then. Please, come in. Do you need some help with the step?"

Due to the cinder blocks, the first and only step into the transportable was a foot and a half off the ground, with the floor of the building another foot and a half past that.

Subconsciously I expected Etta to hike up her skirt and step inside, but she accepted the man's help and clambered up awkwardly. I followed close behind, scared to let her out of my sight.

Dudley was less keen on the idea.

He'd gotten a whole lot better at getting up and down stairs, but this was a long way from normal stairs. Etta and I looked at each other. Since Etta had eaten all the cookies, we didn't have any treats to motivate him with. Failing food, we'd learned there was one other thing that motivated him: high-pitched voices. Embarrassingly high-pitched voices.

We patted our legs and noisily encouraged him the way a parent might exclaim over a kid taking their first steps. He hesitated, so we upped the pitch of our excitement. A second later, he'd eschewed the step altogether and leaped straight into the building.

I caught a glimpse of a smile on Mr. Bergström's face as I turned around. It disappeared without a trace. The way I hoped we weren't about to.

Still, he didn't cut that much of an imposing figure. I was pretty sure between Etta's Glock and my Taser and pepper spray, we could take him. Dudley wouldn't be any help. He didn't have an aggressive bone in his body. I was starting to relax when a dark shape in the far rear of the room, a shape I'd assumed was an armchair, shifted.

The armchair was a man who rivaled Mr. Black in size and bulk. Out of the corner of my eye, I saw him cross his arms.

Okay, if this went wrong, Etta and I were screwed. At least Dudley might have a chance of outrunning them.

I let out a nervous chuckle.

"What can I do for you?" asked Mr. Bergström, drawing our attention back to him.

"It's about one of your employees, sir," Etta said, clinging to her walking stick like she was afraid and the stick was a lifeline. "Abraham Black? He's a big man and a smidge scary to look at, but he's been real kind helping me out over the years. I don't know if you heard, but he got arrested."

Bergström folded his arms too. "Sure, I heard."

"Ah, okay. You might've heard as well that it was because the police thought he murdered somebody. A gentleman you sent him after."

"I heard that's what he said." Bergström's tone was a warning.

One that Etta ignored. "Well, I was wondering if you might tell the police about that. Since he has a young daughter and a wife who'd be awfully upset if he went to jail."

Armchair Man took a step toward us.

"I'm sorry, ladies. But I can't help you."

Etta rummaged in her purse and suddenly had two guns aimed in her direction.

"Don't shoot!" I yelled, causing one of the ugly nozzles to veer my way.

Dudley whined.

"Goodness," Etta said. "I was getting a picture to show you of Abe's lovely wife and their daughter, Joy."

"I'm not interested in seeing it," Bergström said.

"All right. That's all you needed to say." Etta returned the picture to her bag and left her hand where it was. "There's no need to draw weapons when a nice conversation would do. Those things are dangerous, you know."

I held in a cough. Etta wasn't one to lecture on gun restraint.

"I know," said Bergström. "Now I suggest you ladies head on home, and take your dog with you."

We followed his suggestion.

What can I say? It seemed like a good one.

7

IT HADN'T BEEN the most promising start to our investigation, but Etta was undeterred. She pulled out the list Mr. Black had written down for us. The addresses Mr. Bergström had denied ever giving him. "Okay. Let's visit the locations that Michael Watts frequented."

"You don't want to talk about how we almost got shot just now?" I asked.

"Oh, piffle. They were only trying to scare us. Besides, after I put that photo in my purse, I picked up my Glock and had it trained on Bergström ready to go."

I'd been so caught up in her little-old-lady act that it hadn't occurred to me. But that still left two guns against one. A fact I didn't bother to point out, seeing as it would just lead to her making an unflattering comparison between me and a particular type of poultry.

"I need to go to work," I said instead.

Who knew I'd be so pleased to be heading back to the WECS Club? Nothing like having a gun aimed at you to put small-minded politics into perspective.

"I know. I know." Etta sounded annoyed. "But after that. You said you'll be back in a few hours, didn't you?"

Since Connor couldn't make our date, she was regrettably correct. On the other hand, it might be a good thing. By the look of her, she'd be too impatient to wait longer.

"Right," I agreed. "We'll try again when I get back. Don't do anything dangerous without me."

She grunted. Like Connor would have.

What was he doing now? Something even more dangerous than us? He wouldn't be happy to hear about our excursion this morning, especially the bit with the guns.

I checked the rearview mirror all the way home, but it was only when we pulled up to our apartment building without a single glimpse of Armchair Man that I started to feel safe.

"I can't wait to get out of this old-lady outfit," Etta said, her mind apparently on other matters. "It has its uses, but too many hours in this thing and I start to fool myself."

I didn't believe that for a second.

We got out of the car, let Dudley out, and climbed up the stairs together. Etta winked at me before disappearing into her apartment. "Have fun getting dolled up."

Imagining how Etta might envisage my job as a honeytrap kept me entertained while I got dressed and drove to work.

The roses were a great deal more attractive than the metal crushers at my last stop. But like the WECS Club women, their beauty concealed their propensity to inflict harm. I walked through the garden and prepared myself to shield and protect.

There were four members at today's luncheon. While the club was made up of over thirty women, the committee that steered it consisted of just a president, vice president, treasurer, and secretary.

And they despised each other.

Not that there were any overt signs of it in their charming smiles and honeyed tones. But a more experienced eye might notice that the president and vice president had hired Shades, the secretary was claiming morning sickness from a new pregnancy, and the treasurer had begged off eating after a large breakfast and was only pretending to sip her tea. These ladies had trust issues.

Vanessa had told me that all meetings would be held at the clubhouse. Apparently, it was an unspoken rule leading up to the Scandalous Cause photo shoot to never invite anyone home. Three years ago, there'd been some nasty incidents involving hair removal cream finding its way into shampoo and mascara bottles.

It was enough to give any person trust issues.

"How's your open marriage going, Vanessa?" asked the vice president. Miranda, I'd learned her name was. She was dark, sleek, and sharp-clawed like a panther.

"Are you kidding? It's great. I can be with anyone I take a fancy to."

"That's so admirable. I don't know how you do it." That was Stephanie: the blond secretary who looked as if she'd been a playgirl in a former life. She patted her perfectly flat stomach. "Tony is all the man I can handle."

Vanessa cocked her head, making her hair spill over her shoulders in what I was starting to realize was her signature move. "That's one of the best parts about it. I can turn Donald down guilt-free. But I'm glad Tony's enough for you. And you're looking great for being thirteen weeks along. I hope you don't start to show before the shoot."

Stephanie's smile was strained. When the other women's attention wandered, she peeked down at her still-perfectly-flat stomach and frowned.

"Well, I haven't even seen Max for weeks," Miranda said, despite the fact that no one had asked. "He's in Hong Kong closing a multimillion-dollar deal as usual."

"But at least you have the pool boy," Chloe said with a snicker. She was blond as well but had the refined air that came with being born into money. Presumably, as the treasurer, she was good at handling it too.

"I love being my own woman. Not to rain on any of you gals' parade, but freedom, no expectations or compromises, and a fat check from my company every week suits me just fine."

It was an effort to keep my expression neutral. If this was what it meant to be rich and beautiful, I was starting to think being broke and ordinary wasn't such a bad thing.

Vanessa polished off her entree with obvious relish—a dig at those who couldn't eat. "In any case," she said, "I suppose we should get down to business. How many seats do we have left for the Scandalous Cause charity gala?"

I served the next course—a poison-free white truffle risotto—and let my mind wander as they discussed upcoming WECS Club activities.

My eyes stayed pinned on Vanessa's plate.

When she'd eaten, she beckoned me forward and sent me to find a cheese course to finish on. Miranda did the same, so Emily and I went down to the lower level together. I kept to the other side of the stairs in case she decided to give me a helpful shove. She wouldn't, surely, but I felt uneasy all the same. The Mr. Black case must be getting to me.

I'd been hoping to hear gossip about the murder of Michael Watts, but there'd been zilch so far. As I'd feared, the husband of one of their own members being murdered was nothing more than a passing curiosity, and since it had happened days ago, it was old news.

Especially when they needed to one-up each other on their sex lives and plan the seating arrangements for the upcoming gala ball.

The self-absorption was incredible. Then again, until Etta had challenged me on it, I'd been quite happy to go on with my own little life and ignore Mr. Black's plight. Who was I to judge?

We entered the kitchen, and the chef, who'd so far tolerated my intrusion into his domain by acting like I didn't exist, stormed over. "Get out! Get the hell out. And stay out. You can pass your order on to one of my staff and wait in the hall from now on, got it?"

I stared in bewilderment at the outraged man and the knife he was pointing at my nose . . . until Emily piped up.

"Sorry. Chef Rogers was furious that the stove got turned up and ruined his Bordelaise sauce. He was threatening to fire his entire staff, so I had to tell him how I saw you leaning against it earlier. You must have accidentally bumped the control knob."

She was flat out lying. I'd worked around kitchens long enough to never go near the cooking spaces. But Chef

Rogers wasn't going to believe me. I backed into the hall, brain reeling. Emily might not have pushed me down the stairs, but she'd made my job a whole lot harder. Rogers would make sure I had to wait ages for each course until he'd worked off his ill temper or forgotten about me.

Vanessa was not going to be pleased.

Sure enough, Emily waltzed out with her cheese platter before a member of the waitstaff had emerged to even take my order. But the best I could do was obey Chef Roger's demands and hope that staying out of sight would rapidly transition to being out of mind as well.

Eventually a girl came out of the kitchen and grimaced at me sympathetically. "Nothing pisses Rogers off more than a spoiled meal, I'm afraid. What would you like?"

I tested the cheeses, pâté, quince paste, and housemade wafers for poisons as usual but also to make sure Rogers hadn't ruined the taste out of spite. Thankfully, his pride in his work was too great for that.

As I placed the plate in front of Vanessa, her gaze brushed over me. Only for a fraction of a second, but it was long enough to read the message there.

Bad dog.

———

THE WINTER SUN WAS SINKING toward the horizon when Etta and I pulled up to the first of four locations Michael Watts used to frequent before he was murdered.

We'd left Dudley snoozing at home and were in my car. A silver Corvette was less noticeable than a yellow Dodge Charger, and there was a possibility it would be best not to attract attention. Etta was back in her normal clothes, figuring anyone the wealthy Michael Watts hung out with would respond better to style than sweetness.

In front of us was an unremarkable-looking house on an upper-middle-class suburban street in Oakwood. It was late afternoon—hardly prime time for thugs or shady dealings—but I was apprehensive anyway.

Etta unbuckled her seat belt before I'd killed the engine and slipped out the door. "What are you waiting for?"

I wondered how she'd lived so long with such a penchant for risk taking.

"What if it's an arms dealer?" I asked, then realized that might excite her further. "Or a grieving friend?"

"Hopefully, it's the first of those options. That would be interesting."

It seemed wrong that hanging out with a woman in her seventies made me feel old, but it did. I held back a sigh and followed her to the front door.

A lady about Etta's age opened it. The pair of them seemed to be cut from the same cloth—both elegant and stylishly dressed. Her gaze swept dismissively over me but lingered on Etta. "Ooh. You look like you have spice. Who referred you?"

"Michael Watts," Etta said.

"Well, all right then. Come on in. I'm Madam Devine in case my reputation has failed to precede me. For future visits, drive up to the garage and our security will let you in. There's a private parking area out the back."

Etta nudged me. "Oh good," I said. "I was worried about leaving the car out the front."

Madam Devine ushered us into a sitting room featuring red-and-gold wallpaper, dark timber furniture, and a mocha-colored velour couch she directed us toward. We sank deep into it like chocolate chips into cake batter. I hoped we'd be able to get up again without assistance.

Devine's chair looked much firmer, and she sat on it primly. "Now we're comfortable, let's go over your personal tastes and appetites. I specialize in finding the ideal fit for every client." She smiled, and I hid a wince at the double meaning of her words. "So, what are you into?"

Etta and I looked at each other. At this point, I was guessing the establishment provided services of a sexual nature, but that meant the range of potential options was as broad as Santa's backside. And I had no doubt that if we answered incorrectly, the security she'd mentioned would throw us out on our asses. We'd have to keep it as vague as possible and hope her responses would help us nut it out.

No pun intended.

I giggled like a teenager in a sex ed. class. "Sorry. We've never done this before. Um. Where do we start?"

Devine kept her smile pasted on, but her eyes were shuttered, utterly bored. "Are you interested in booking together or separately?"

"Separately," Etta said. "I'll go first. I've had more years to figure out what I want than this young whippersnapper."

The boredom lifted, just a touch. "And what is it you want?" she purred.

I hoped Etta knew what she was doing.

"Everything."

"An excellent choice. But where would you like to start?" Her spiked foot bounced impatiently.

"Something spicy. Like you guessed."

"What kind of spice?"

This woman wasn't giving us anything. Was she suspicious?

"I think I'll start with Michael's brand of spice," Etta said. "That's what encouraged me to come in the first place."

I mentally applauded her. It would make sense to Madam Devine even when we didn't know what it was, and we might learn more about what our victim was into. And whether someone might want to kill him for it.

"Really?" Devine looked surprised. I was guessing she was rarely surprised. "It's unusual for a woman to be into that."

Uh-oh.

"I've lived a long time and tried a lot of things. I know what I like. Normal gets boring after a while."

"Great. I'll go and get the security boys to bring up a forty-four-gallon drum and get the girls to prepare the room for you. I'll be back in a moment."

Forty-four-gallon drum?

She disappeared from view, and I leaped up, trying to pull Etta with me. "Let's go. We have to get out of here!"

"Don't be silly. We might get the same sex worker Michael used, and they could tell us more."

"They might not want to talk," I hissed, still trying to pull her out of the stupid, spongy couch.

She refused to move, giving me no choice but to sit my butt down and act normal at the sound of returning heels on the floorboards.

"And what about you?" Madam Devine asked me.

My cheeks heated, and my brain seized. I had nothing. This was way out of my comfort zone, and I wasn't a great actress at the best of times.

"We've talked it over," Etta said. "For today, she'll join us. Or at least she'll come and watch."

Gross. But it did get me out of fabricating up some kind of kinky sexual fantasy in front of these two worldly women. I was sure to embarrass myself.

"No problem," Devine said like we were discussing job orientation, "but voyeurism does cost extra. I'm sure Michael would've told you we take cash up front, so that'll be three thousand dollars."

Etta shot out of the spongy chair. "Of course, but I was having a look, and my purse must've fallen out in the car. We'll be right back."

This time, she grabbed me and we hotfooted it to the car. I jumped into the cool leather seat with a sense of escaping a fate worse than death and cranked the engine. Throwing caution to the wind, I started driving before I finished buckling up my seat belt. That's how scared I was of watching Etta with a sex worker and a forty-four-gallon drum.

I checked the rearview mirror to see if Madam Devine had sent one of her security staff after us. I'd been checking the rearview mirror a lot today. It was clear of pursuers, but we'd burned that bridge and would get no further information from Madam's house of whorish horrors.

I couldn't convince myself it was a bad thing. What on earth had I gotten myself into?

"Okay," I said, checking the mirror once more. "So our victim was into strange sex involving forty-four-gallon drums and paid for it. That could give someone a reason to kill him, right?"

"Yes, mostly his wife."

"Oh. Yeah." I didn't want the wife to be our primary suspect. If she was, we'd have to confront her, and if we were wrong, we'd be harassing a genuinely grieving widow.

I chewed my lip. "What would one do with forty-four-gallon drums?"

Etta popped a tab of nicotine gum into her mouth and looked at me sideways. "Are you sure you want to know the answer to that?"

I thought about it.

"Maybe just tell me what the next address is."

8

MICHAEL WATTS'S company headquarters revealed no clues about the fate of its CEO.

The company operated from the top two floors of a twelve-story building in Downtown LA. We did a drive-by inspection, but it wasn't easy to gawk at from the road. Our chances of convincing someone to give us a tour at this late hour were slim, and the chances of digging up sordid secrets under the watchful eye of a tour guide even more so. We opted to move on.

That left one location to go—just one more chance to find a concrete lead for solving the case—because the fourth address on Mr. Black's list was the Watts' home we'd seen this morning.

I couldn't believe that had only been this morning.

We stopped outside a swanky bar in Hollywood Heights and made our way inside. It was dimly lit, with candles on each of the tables and a few strategically placed hanging bulbs to stop you from bumping into things. The building must have been a family residence in a former life, and its haphazard layout with many rooms gave the place a private, boutique vibe. An eclectic collection of art on the walls and brown leather couches positioned to take advantage of every nook added to the ambience.

It was early enough that the bar was almost empty. A bartender was restocking the cocktail ingredients, so we pulled up stools and ordered gin and tonics.

I'd earned half a dozen gin and tonics today.

The bartender had the special Los Angeles air of someone who was biding time until he caught his big break. He paid more attention to deciding whether we were anyone important than making our drinks, and he set our glasses down with a halfhearted smile. Not important then.

I slid my phone over to him anyway. "Do you remember seeing this man here?"

He looked over the photo of Michael, up at us again, then back at the photo. "Sure, he was a regular, but I saw on the news he was shot in his own home. Something wrong with that isn't there? What did you wanna know?"

Maybe he figured there was a chance we were reporters

and he'd get some free publicity. Maybe he was bored.

"How often was he here?"

"I'd guess two or three times a week."

"Did he ever meet with anyone?"

"Don't think I ever saw him alone. But he met with someone different almost every night. Used to sit in that corner over there."

As helpful as he was being, it made me miss my housemate Oliver who also happened to be a bartender. He would've found a way to make me choke on my drink by now with his usual antics.

"Were they always women?" Etta asked.

We were only fifteen minutes from Madam Devine's home. Perhaps he took his dates here—before or after whatever they did with those drums.

"No. It would've been an even split I reckon," the man told us, surreptitiously checking his reflection in the glass he was polishing.

Unless our victim was bisexual, that made it sound like business. But the bar didn't seem the kind of place his associates in the sports industry would favor. We asked our star-in-waiting a few more questions but failed to uncover the big clue we'd been searching for. I hoped he'd have more luck catching his big break.

Driving home, we ran through what we'd learned since my online stalking of our victim this morning. Michael

Watts's life was not as perfect as his social media and PR company liked to portray.

Even aside from the being dead thing.

"So according to our nosy neighbor—"

"You mean Mr. Nostril Hairs," Etta corrected.

"Right. According to him, a woman was watching and following our victim a week before he was killed. Do you think she could've been a private investigator hired by his suspicious wife? Maybe she found out about his expensive sexual activities like we did."

"Could be. Or it might've been a sex worker he paid to stalk him as part of one of his fantasies. I heard that some people have a fetish for—"

"That's one possibility," I said, not wanting to hear the end of that sentence. "Otherwise it could have been a stakeholder in the company he was struggling to keep afloat, looking for dirt to remove him from the management board. Or a way of removing him more permanently."

"Sure. Or maybe she was an innocent passerby who got lost and was struggling to figure out how to use her GPS."

Ugh. I hoped not. The woman in the car was the one scenario we'd uncovered where someone aside from the victim was acting suspiciously.

"Then there's all his after-hours meetings with different people in a dimly lit bar," Etta said. "Whatever he got up to on those two or three nights a week, I'm guessing it wasn't good."

"I agree, but vaguely questionable activity isn't going to sway the police."

We were both quiet for a bit.

"Why do you think the killer chose to shoot him in the head?" I asked. "As far as I understand, it's a smaller and therefore harder target to hit, so you'd need to have a reason for shooting there."

Etta shrugged. "It's got one of the best fatality rates as far as body parts go. So it makes sense unless you're a crap shot."

"I think your idea of a crap shot might vary from normal people's." I'd been to a shooting range with her and my aunt and discovered she was a superb shot. Better than Connor even. "A normal person might aim for the head out of rage though, to make his hated face disappear."

"Or if they weren't any good at shooting, maybe they did it for target practice."

I was glad Etta was one of a kind. The notion of a murderer choosing how to kill based on improving their skill set was unsettling. And it wasn't even the reason I was feeling ill at ease . . .

For a day's work by two amateur sleuths, we'd found out a lot. The problem was none of the pieces fit together or so much as pointed strongly in one direction. Worse, we were out of leads and resources.

The Black family's happiness was hanging in the balance, and I had no idea where to go from here.

———

MEOW MISSED OLIVER, I decided as I watched her halfheartedly bat away at a dead cockroach. I'd never seen her play with a dead one; it was the live ones that got her excited. She would place the lifeless bodies in a neat little pile of victory and leave them alone after that. And I'd never seen her play so unenthusiastically either. Would a Skype conversation with him help?

"Don't be sad, sweetie. He's coming home soon."

She left the cockroach discarded on the linoleum, two feet from her pile—another anomaly—and made her way over to me. I picked her up and carried her to my bedroom.

"You should be glad I'm not offended," I told her. "Since I feed you and let you steal my pillow even when I'm trying to use it. Did I mention the crick I had in my neck this morning?"

I sat on the bed, and she kneaded my legs while I rubbed her in her favorite spots. That reminded me, I needed to replace my pillowcase and matching duvet cover. Of all the used household items I'd inherited from former tenants when I'd moved in, the duvet cover was the most hideous. It was one thing to be wise with money, it was another to start the new year—the year I was going to turn thirty—with rainbow-vomit bedding.

Or maybe I was getting snobby after hanging out with Connor? I looked at my Ugg boots and sweats. Nope, probably not.

"What should I replace it with?" Tiny gray and black hairs floated down from where I scratched Meow under the chin. "Perhaps a plain charcoal color to camouflage your fur?"

She seemed to approve of that, because she finished kneading and lay down at last, purring like it was going out of fashion. And on the subject of out-of-fashion things—regardless of my dislike of shopping, I was going to replace my duvet cover before the end of the year.

I wrote myself a reminder and wondered if that could count as a New Year's resolution. Between my job, my new boyfriend, and my extracurricular activities with Etta, I didn't have the time or energy to tackle something else.

Although right now I had time, and I was trying hard not to think about how Connor hadn't answered any of my texts. Or how far Etta and I were from casting doubt on Mr. Black's guilt, let alone proving his innocence.

Etta had stayed silent on the way home. Either she'd come to the same heavy conclusion I had, or she'd been entertaining herself with notions of forty-four-gallon drums. I hadn't asked which.

My phone rang, and I grabbed it eagerly, hoping it might be Connor. But the number was unknown.

"Ms. Avery? It's Joy here. Abraham Black's daughter. I'm not supposed to be calling, but I'm worried about my parents and I was wondering how you were going with the case?"

The weight on my shoulders got an awful lot heavier. Knowing she was a smart kid, I tried to inject optimism into my tone. "It's going well so far. We have some promising leads," I said, stretching the truth like it was melted mozzarella.

"What kind of leads?"

Damn.

"Well, it's still early, but we know he was involved in at least one uh, frowned-upon activity and that someone else was following him shortly before he died."

"Okay. Good. Because Mr. Bergström, that's Dad's boss if you didn't remember, came around today and fired Dad. He hated that job, but it's the only one he had, and with the murder charge hanging over his head, he's real concerned he won't be able to get another one. Not that he admitted it to me of course, but I can see straight through him."

I experienced a sinking sensation in the pit of my stomach.

"And then Principal Gibson came around to talk about how to handle everything when school starts up again. Dad's name was in the paper as a murder suspect, and Principal Gibson knew the other kids will give me hell over it. She was trying to help, but I think it made Dad feel even worse."

I hadn't considered that side of things. From what Joy had told me, she wasn't popular at the pretentious school to start with.

"Anyway," Joy continued, "I guess I was just hoping to hear that progress is being made. It's best for my parents' health that this goes away as soon as possible."

"Sure," I said, trying to keep my positive tone afloat. Unable to think of anything better, I borrowed a line from the TV detectives. "We'll do everything we can."

It seemed to satisfy her because she said goodbye and hung up.

I sank back into the couch with Meow, my stomach and shoulders feeling heavy now. What if our visit to Bergström today had gotten Mr. Black fired?

Lucky the new year hadn't arrived yet, or I'd be off to a very bad start.

9

CONNOR TEXTED ME THE NEXT morning and asked if I could meet him for breakfast. On the drive there, I rehearsed how I'd break the news of the case.

"Do you want the good or the bad news first?" I'd smile charmingly so he'd remember that he liked me—really he did—before I continued. "The good news is, I've gone back to carrying my Taser and pepper spray around with me all the time."

He'd be pleased to hear I was taking self-protective measures.

"The bad news is I agreed to help Etta and we got held at gunpoint yesterday. But they didn't shoot."

Hmm. That he would be less pleased about.

"You know that case you told me absolutely not to take? Um . . . we both know I'm not great at saying no, right?"

Perhaps I could put a better spin on it.

"Remember when you said that you admire how I look for the good in people?"

No. He wouldn't appreciate having his compliment used against him. Especially when I got to the guns part.

"The bad news is I agreed to help Etta exactly how you told me not to. The good news is, I don't want to talk about it, so we can go and ravish each other as soon as we're done here."

Yeah, maybe I'd go with that last one.

Connor was late. Which was almost unheard of, and when he arrived, he was wound as tight as Aunt Alice watching me drink from one of her precious crystal glasses. I could have been imagining it, but even his close-cropped hair seemed a touch scruffy. His embrace was still strong and warm, but his kiss was brusque.

"Are you okay?" I asked.

"Of course. Sorry I'm late." He didn't offer an explanation as to why, and his mask was firmly in place.

"It's no problem. Just gives me an excuse to drink more coffee." I grinned, but he didn't look at me to notice it. "Are you sure you're okay? What happened yesterday?"

"Let's talk about something else. How's your new client going?"

I would've preferred to talk about him, but I answered the question in the hope that my sharing would encourage his own.

"Interesting. I've never witnessed so much insincerity in my life. There are always two different conversations going on. If you read a transcript of it, you'd think they were kind and sweet, but when you can hear their voices and see their facial expressions and body language, it's another conversation entirely."

Connor was staring at the menu, unresponsive.

I slipped it gently away from him. "Something's wrong." I stated it as fact rather than asking him, hoping he might stop denying it. Might elaborate.

He did neither. "Sorry. This was a bad idea. Can I leave you to eat alone?"

"Um. Sure," I said, wishing he'd speak to me but not wanting to force the issue.

He stood up, and I felt a flash of dread, quickly stifled.

Stuff it. I'd ask him outright rather than stew over it for however long it took him to talk.

"It's . . . not about us, is it?"

His gray eyes caught mine for the first time today. "No. I'll see you later."

For a minute after he left, I sat there, sipping my coffee,

wondering whether I still had an appetite for breakfast. A waitress passed carrying poached eggs with pulled pork, hollandaise sauce, and salsa.

Of course I still had an appetite.

———

IT HAD BEEN FIFTEEN YEARS since I'd visited the principal's office. The last occasion had been about some chocolate pudding sauce that had mysteriously ended up on my bully's chair, which my bully had then sat in. I was hoping this one would go better.

I glanced at my companion and experienced a flicker of doubt that it would.

She was dressed to impress in an ensemble of the most expensive clothes we owned. Her dress was Neiman Marcus, something she'd splurged on when she'd found it in a secondhand shop. Even secondhand it was almost more than she could justify. The shoes were Kate Spade. A gift from an admirer. And the jacket was one that Connor's stylist had purchased for me when I'd worked as his Shade—part of an enforced makeover to bring me up to scratch with his public image. I'd since learned that most of that enforced makeover thing had been a farce, but I wasn't sure how he felt about my general lack of style. Neither Etta nor I had a bag that would pass muster, so we'd left them behind.

I was dressed in smart business attire, also thanks to Connor's stylist. A pencil skirt that was doing its darnedest to strangle my waist, and a loose-fitting silk blouse. While we'd done nothing to change our faces beyond normal makeup, the outfits were deliberately chosen to help our story fly, and Etta was ecstatic to be wearing "disguises" and going "undercover." Her enthusiasm made me nervous. A lot of things about Etta made me nervous.

The Frederick Academy was a proud three-story, red-brick building with cream accents and pristine lawns. We made our way to the school reception, and I let Etta do the talking.

"I'm here to see Principal Gibson," she announced imperiously to the woman behind the polished timber desk.

"Of course, ma'am. What time was your appointment?"

Joy's phone call last night had given me the idea to seek out the principal. Because both the victim and the suspect were parents at her school, I figured she'd be stuck doing damage control. And since she was keeping abreast of the case, she might offer a unique perspective on the whole thing. If we could get past her receptionist guard and convince her to talk to us.

That's what the clothes were for.

Etta pulled herself taller. "I wouldn't think patrons of this school as generous as my family would need an appointment."

The receptionist was unimpressed. Probably used to powerful, entitled parents pushing her around. "I'm sorry, ma'am, but I'm not allowed to let anyone by without an appointment. Perhaps if you give me your name, I can see if she'll make an exception for you?"

"Mrs. Yale," Etta said, naming the family we'd chosen to impersonate since I'd overheard mention of their significant donations. "I'm Timmy's grandmother, and this is my personal aide, Isobel."

The woman's eyes narrowed. "That's funny. I had the good fortune of speaking with Mrs. Yale at the gala dinner last month."

Oops.

"Ah yes, you would have. My apologies, I should've been more clear." Etta's tone suggested the receptionist should've been less dense. "I'm Mr. Yale's father's sister, which makes Timmy technically my grandnephew, but we're so close he calls me grandmother."

Wow. Etta was good at this. She would make a way better Shade than I did. A much better honeytrap too.

The receptionist stapled some papers together. "Oh, I hadn't heard the good news." Her voice was chirpy, but there was an off-key ring to it that made me sense a setup.

"Good news?" asked Timmy's alleged great-aunt.

"That Mr. Yale Senior found a sister he never knew about. The Yale family has been sending their children to this school for four generations, and Anthony Yale was an only child, at least according to our records." She crunched the stapler again for emphasis, the way a judge uses a gavel, then picked up the phone. "Now, would you like to leave, or shall I call security?"

"We'll be on our way," I said, just as two burly men burst through the doors, SECURITY in bold letters across their chest. They grabbed my arm, and I flicked a questioning glance at the receptionist.

She smiled. "Forgive me for misleading you. I have a discreet little button I can press with my knee to call these lovely men in here. Also, I've taken a photo of you both and will be handing it out to all security personnel. So don't come back okay?" Her fingers were tapping away at the keyboard before we'd been hauled through the front doors. Apparently, our exit wasn't even worth watching.

———

AFTER WE'D BEEN ESCORTED off the Frederick Academy grounds, Etta let go of the rich and powerful act and popped some gum into her mouth. "We would've gotten away with it if our intel wasn't bad," she griped.

Intel meaning the family name I'd given her. "How was I supposed to know the receptionist sees the grandparents at gala dinners?"

Etta shrugged. "It doesn't matter now."

I glanced over at her. It wasn't like Etta to sound dispirited, and I felt a wave of compassion. "Is this investigation getting you down?"

Our efforts hadn't been encouraging so far. Maybe it didn't seem so fun anymore.

"Pah. I'm annoyed you don't have more time to work on it today. I know we can't all be retired and free, but I was hoping this morning's lead would pay off so I'd at least have something exciting to chew over until tonight."

Right. I should've known the only thing that bothered Etta was boredom.

Between my failed breakfast with Connor, a lunch date with Harper, and a long WECS Club function this afternoon, I was having to squeeze the case in between appointments. Pointing out to my investigation partner that we didn't have any leads left anyway wasn't going to help. "I'll call you as soon as I'm free this evening," I promised instead.

Besides, maybe I'd overhear some pivotal gossip at the WECS Club that would bring about a break in the case. Or maybe the Black family should've gotten a professional PI to investigate on their behalf.

I dropped Etta back to our apartment building and drove to meet Harper. Unfortunately, being alone in the car gave me an opportunity to think about Connor.

Despite asking him outright about his unusual behavior this morning, my gut knotted with anxiety whenever my mind returned to it. Whatever was behind it, I'd never seen him so . . . distressed. That was the word. It scared me to imagine what might unsettle Connor so badly. Not bloody much. The worst part was he wouldn't let me near him to help.

I'd love to ask Harper if she knew what was wrong, but chances were good she wouldn't have any more answers than me. His family didn't even know as much as I did— that the Taste Society existed and he worked for them. I resolved to keep my fears to myself.

Harper worked at an automotive repair shop in Silver Lake. I found a nearby parking space after a mere four laps around the block, located the faded red-and-white sign she'd told me to look out for, and entered the open garage. It was cooler inside than out and smelled of new tires, gasoline, and cleaning supplies. "Harper?"

Her legs emerged from under the Toyota Tacoma I was standing beside and startled the wits out of me. Luckily, it took another second for her head to appear so she didn't see me jump.

"Izzy! Thanks so much for meeting me here." She bounced to her feet. "Hang on, let me get these overalls off so I don't get you all filthy when we hug." Under the navy overalls, she was in shorts and tank top, despite the winter season. Her long, dark hair was tied out of the way in a messy plait, and a smudge of dirt lined one of her cheeks.

I wondered whether I had powdered sugar on mine from the apple strudel I'd picked up en route. Comfort food for the Connor thing.

She wrapped me in a dust, oil, and violet-scented hug. "I thought we should get to know each other since you're the first girl my brother's shown interest in for I don't know how long. The test results came back clear this afternoon, if you hadn't heard by the way."

"Wait. Test results?"

"Mom's. Don't tell me Connor didn't tell you?" She studied my face. "He didn't tell you. Ugh. I warned you he has the social skills of a club-dragging Neanderthal, didn't I? Mom went to the hospital early yesterday morning with chest pain. They treat that kind of thing very seriously of course. But they've scanned every inch of her heart and it's as healthy as can be. So nothing to be concerned about. Not that Connor would take the doctor's word for it. He's being his overprotective self and demanding Mom stay with him for a while. Are you okay? I'm sorry to break the news to you like this."

I was reeling in shock. And hurt. How could he keep this from me? What did he think I was going to do with the news? Sell it to the media? If he didn't trust me to help him through this, what did that say about the future of our relationship? That was the crux of the problem. The core of my hurt. But it wasn't Harper I needed to take it up with. I pushed the whole mess aside and focused on the woman in front of me.

"No need to be sorry. It took me by surprise, that's all. But I'm so glad Mae's going to be fine! That deserves another hug."

Harper chuckled and hugged me again. I couldn't help but compare that to Connor, who I'd never heard laugh. Snort in amusement once or twice, but never laugh. What would it sound like? Did he ever let his guard down enough to do that with anyone?

"How did you and Connor evolve from the same upbringing?" I asked.

Her gray eyes, the same shade as her brother's, sparkled. I'd never seen his do that either. "I've often wondered about that," she told me. "But we were night and day from the beginning. I'd be hammering my toy cars together in brilliant smash-ups worthy of an action film, and he'd ask me what happened to the people inside. Mom eventually came up with a story about how the cars were remote controlled, which seemed to satisfy him, but he was a solemn kid. And Dad passing away didn't do anything to help that. But he's become even more closed off over the years. I think his work, with all its classified stuff and seeing the bad side of human nature over and over again has made it worse. That's why Mom and I were so relieved when he brought you home and you turned out to have a sense of fun. He needs that in his life."

"Well, thank you."

She waved a hand. "Pfft, thanks for putting up with him, and I'm happy to give you the inside gossip on Connor, but today I'd like to get to know you better. Let's get some food first though. I'm starving."

"Then you and I should get along great."

We walked a few blocks to a simple, homey café called Modern Eats and seated ourselves by the window.

"What kind of car do you drive?" Harper asked. "I can tell a lot about a person by their car."

"A twelve-year-old Corvette, but it's a company car. I love it, if that's helpful to know. Before that, I used to drive an ancient Ford Fairlane. I called her Gerry, short for Geriatric. What does that tell you?"

"That you used to be broke and you know nothing about cars."

I laughed. "Correct on both counts. What clued you in?"

"Older Ford Fairlanes are unreliable gas guzzlers. I bet ol' Gerry broke down on you at least three times. And the electrics are worse. You either spend a small fortune on upkeep or get used to not having any windows or central locking. The buying price is cheap, but it's what they call a false economy. And the 'vettes are pretty reliable, but since it's a company car, I'm not giving you any credit for that one."

I nodded. "That's impressive, but I can tell a lot about a person by the way they order food."

"Really? Let's order then, and you can tell me all about myself. This is going to be fun."

By the time I left lunch with Harper, I was starting to think I was dating the wrong sibling.

10

I PHONED CONNOR as soon as I was out of earshot.

Lucky for him, he picked up. Or maybe it wasn't lucky. Maybe I should've waited to get over my hurt a bit first.

I skipped the niceties and jumped straight to the point. "So I met with Harper just now, and she told me what's been going on with Mae."

"Right."

"What I don't understand is why you didn't tell me about it," I said, trying to keep my tone very reasonable under the circumstances.

"I didn't think it was relevant."

Staying reasonable was going to be harder than I'd thought. "Didn't think it was relevant? Of course it's relevant! I care about you, and I care about your family." Harper's words echoed through my head. "I know it might be hard for you to be vulnerable, but if we're going to do this, you need to let me in."

He didn't respond.

"You do want to do this, right?"

"Yes."

That word, at least, seemed sincere. The pressure eased from around my chest.

"Well . . . good. You know, I can't tell if you're deliberately being obtuse or you really don't understand how relationships are supposed to work."

"Can't it be both?"

If we'd been together, I would've hit him. Sure, it might have been more painful for me than him, but it would have been satisfying. Instead, I had to content myself with groaning.

He didn't respond, of course.

"How is she?" I asked.

"Who?"

"You're being deliberately obtuse again. How's your mom?"

"She thinks I should stop being a nuisance and let her go home."

"I agree with her. That you should stop being a nuisance that is. Not that you should let her go home."

Connor snorted. "And you wonder why I don't tell you anything."

"Uh-uh. You can't turn this around on me. You're the one with communication issues, and the first step to dealing with it is accepting you have a problem." I paused. "Do you? Accept that I mean?"

It took a very long time for him to reply. "I accept that you think I have a problem."

Ugh. "Seriously? I'm pretty sure you'd feel differently if the shoe was on the other foot. You have a GPS tracker on my phone, surveillance on my front door, and a partner who tells you things." I felt a twinge of guilt at the last one since I still hadn't told him about Mr. Black's case. Then again, I hadn't had the chance to either. "That's a lot of information," I pointed out. "How would you feel if I disconnected all that stuff and stopped talking to you?"

"That's different. It's about your safety."

"It's the exact same thing. You care about my safety and well-being, and I care about yours. But that goes beyond the physical, so when your mom is in the hospital, both your and her well-being are at stake, and I want to be there for you. Which I can't do if I you don't tell me about it."

Connor grunted. It didn't even sound like an affirmative grunt.

"It's not like I'll be any good at protecting you physically,"

I persisted, "so this is it. This is the way I can be your partner and support you. But you need to let me."

Silence.

"Look, I have to go, but think about this, okay? This is not just a difference of opinion, this is a foundational element of having a relationship, and while I don't expect you to turn into Chatty Cathy, you need to learn to share things with me."

He grunted again.

"I'm going to take that to mean you'll think about it. Lovely speaking with you."

Okay, the last sentence might've been sarcastic. But while I consider myself a patient person (except when I'm hungry), Connor was a sore test of that particular virtue.

————

AN HOUR LATER, I was standing once more in the WECS Club ballroom. I used one of the grand white columns to steady myself. Partly because of the inappropriate heels my client expected me to wear and partly because I was juggling three missions: fulfill my Shade duties, observe and eavesdrop to collect useful information for Vanessa, and obtain a new lead on the Watts case.

The Taste Society wouldn't be happy about that if they ever found out. Keeping Vanessa Madison poison-free in this den of iniquity was more than enough to keep my full attention.

I strode over and grabbed the glass that I'd seen one of her companions' hand hover over. "May I get you something more suitable for the next course, Mrs. Madison?"

She fluttered a hand at me without sparing a glance. Now how could I ensure no one poisoned her food while I was gone? I couldn't, so I grabbed her plate too. She'd only eaten three bites of it.

Knowing she was safe, albeit without any food or drink, I took my time wandering through the crowd on my way to the kitchen, listening for interesting snippets of conversation.

"You'll never believe what I caught my maid doing."

I resisted my natural curiosity and didn't slow down to find out.

"It doesn't matter. René Laurent chooses whoever puts out most satisfactorily."

Here I paused. René Laurent was the fashion mogul who determined which of the twelve photos made the cut into the Scandalous Cause calendar. Vanessa might want to know about this one.

"No way, everyone knows he's gay," the woman's companion replied.

"Then maybe they send their husbands." Snickers of laughter. I moved on.

"I heard they arrested someone already."

"Was it his wife? By the sounds of it, she had plenty of reasons to want to kill him."

What kind of reasons?

"No, she had an alibi. It was another parent at the Frederick Academy apparently. The father of one of those scholarship kids from a low socioeconomic background. Beats me why they let the little troublemakers rub shoulders with the leaders of the future."

It was tempting to trip and send Vanessa's wine all over the snobby, self-entitled witch, but I was supposed to stay invisible. Plus I had to test the wine to confirm whether it had been spiked.

I traipsed back down the stairs toward the kitchen and tasted it as soon as I was out of sight. Poisoned with lithin and celandium, two innocuous over-the-counter drugs that when mixed together with alcohol would've given Vanessa a nasty, acne-like rash. How did these women learn this stuff? Was there a convenient little handbook on how to poison your friends?

I'd have to study the WECS Club member whose hand passed over the glass so I could describe her to Vanessa and earn my extra cash. But before that, thanks to Emily and the would-be poisoner, I'd get to repeat the entire rigmarole of waiting long minutes outside the kitchen for new food, testing said food, and watching hawk-eyed as

Vanessa attempted to eat it.

With the next course in hand, I was halfway through the crowd when a hush went over the room. All eyes swiveled to the staircase. A dainty brunette had just reached the top. She wore a simple black shift dress that skimmed the floor as she walked. I wondered who she was to command so much interest. Not even Vanessa Madison had such a physical effect on the club.

"Nicole, how are you holding up?" asked a woman in a fitted skirt and cashmere wrap. The spell on the room broke. Conversations resumed. I heard whispers of "widow" and remembered where I'd seen her before. Michael Watts's wife.

One of our primary suspects.

Nothing about her suggested she knew her way around a gun. She was quiet and withdrawn, in a manner that seemed more habitual than a new state of grief. But you never knew what was going on beneath the surface, especially with the quiet types.

Maybe she'd found out about her husband's dirty secrets and had been planning the murder for weeks. Maybe she'd been waiting for an opportunity. And maybe Mr. Black had given it to her. When she came home to find Michael badly beaten, she could've finished it right then so there might be someone else to take the blame. Sure, they'd said she had an alibi, but alibis could be bought.

Nicole sank into a seat as if she couldn't stand up any longer, and I realized I was staring. I resumed my way over to my client and felt bad for thinking like that about someone who was probably genuinely mourning the loss of her life partner. But that's what detectives did, I guess. Think the worst of people. No wonder Connor wasn't good at relationships.

I shifted my mind back to my three missions. I had my hands full without throwing Connor into the mix.

By the time Vanessa decided she was ready to depart, my feet were aching again and the only missions I'd achieved were the ones she'd set me. Priority parking was given to the WECS Club members, leaving "the help" with a long walk to their vehicles over pebbled paths. It was a lovely stroll through the garden but painful in heels. So after the first WECS function, I'd brought a pair of comfy shoes to change into for the trek to and from the parking lot.

I hobbled into the walk-in closet where the working staff stored their belongings and slipped off my heels with giddy relief. Barefoot, I rummaged through my bag and then rummaged some more. What the heck? My comfy shoes were missing. It was easy enough to lose something small in the cavernous properties of my bag, but shoes were another matter. And sure, my eyes were fatigued, but not that fatigued. I checked the cubbyhole my stuff had been stowed in, but it was empty too. There was only one explanation.

Emily Lin.

We'd left at similar times yesterday. So much so that I'd all but power walked to my car to avoid a long, awkward stroll beside her. She must have seen my efficient, clever shoe system and hatched up this foul plot.

I leaned my head against the wall and wondered what I'd done to deserve an enemy like her. I'd been trying to take the high road, hoping my lack of reaction would make her feel guilty or lose interest. But enough was enough. She was going to learn that two could play her vindictive games. I thought I'd grown out of that sort of thing after graduating high school, but it turned out that adults could be equally petty and childish. Maybe more so.

Mind turning over revenge strategies, I pulled my blasted heels back on and headed to the parking lot. I tried to enjoy the green lawns and rose bushes, but it was hard with a blister developing on each of my little toes. When I finally saw my Corvette's silver nose peeking out from the other cars, the "Hallelujah Chorus" played in my mind.

Until I went to grab my keys.

She wouldn't.

I sat down on a patch of grass and pulled every last item out of my bag.

She did. She'd taken my keys as well.

I couldn't imagine her actually stealing them. Grand theft auto wasn't her style. Petty aggravation was. Which meant that she'd probably hidden them somewhere in the stupid closet I'd just come from. On the off-chance I was wrong, I could hardly call someone to come to my rescue until I knew for sure.

I said a naughty word.

It was sorely tempting to walk back in bare feet, but Vanessa wouldn't appreciate the scandal if I was caught. I grumbled and limped all the way to the clubhouse, then began a systematic search of the cubbyholes.

The door to the closet opened as I was looking behind someone else's bag.

"What are you doing? That's Chantelle's bag."

I spun, feeling guilty even though I wasn't doing anything wrong. It was the girl who'd been sympathetic after the chef had kicked me out of the kitchen. She wasn't looking sympathetic now.

"I seem to have misplaced my car keys, and I'm trying to find them."

"Why would they end up in someone else's cubbyhole?"

Great. Now if anything went missing from anyone's bags, I'd be branded a thief as well as a meal-destroyer. I'd like to think Emily wouldn't go that far, but I wasn't sure anymore. I ran through my options quickly and decided to tell this girl the truth. That way if something did go missing, maybe I'd have at least one person on my side.

"To be honest, the new girl that's working for the vice president has it in for me. I think she turned up the stove on purpose and blamed it on me, and now she's hidden my keys and the comfy shoes I wear to and from the parking lot."

The girl looked unconvinced. "That sounds kinda far-fetched, but I'm sorry if it's true. I guess we'll know by whether anyone's missing their belongings tomorrow." She shot me a meaningful look, then grabbed her bag and left.

I groaned and resumed my search.

11

I FINALLY LOCATED BOTH THE KEYS and shoes hidden behind someone else's bag and drove home half an hour later than I'd expected. Etta was almost bouncing with impatience.

"Where have you been? I followed the principal after work to see if she went anywhere we could talk to her. And she went to a local bar without that snotty receptionist, but I don't know how long she'll stay, so we have to go right now!"

"You followed her? Alone? I thought we were doing this case together. What if she was dangerous? Even professional detectives have a partner for safety."

"She's the principal for goodness' sake, and I followed her discreetly from a distance. The most dangerous part of the whole thing was the possibility of a traffic collision. Now let's go."

I knew she'd leave without me if I didn't relent, so I trudged down the stairs. "We'll go in my car then. I don't know how anyone can be discreet in a car the color of Tweety Bird."

Etta opted not to answer that. She gave me directions, and I started driving. Somewhere along the way, I noticed she was wearing her little-old-lady costume again.

"I'm not sure about that outfit," I told her. "So far it's left me abandoned to Commander Hunt's less-than-tender mercies and gotten us almost shot at."

"Nonsense, dear. This outfit is capable of miracles."

Good. We were going to need one.

It was a modest establishment, the type that caters to the local regulars rather than tourists or those looking for a fun, new experience. Our target was sitting alone by the bar, nursing an amber-colored liquid that could've been scotch . . . or apple juice. I was betting on the alcohol. There wasn't much else on offer in a place like this.

Her clothing was tailored and looked expensive, but somehow she didn't give off the same impression as most of the WECS Club women. As if the picture of prosperity was a mirage that kept flickering around the edges.

Etta shambled along in her little-old-lady outfit. The transformation went deeper than the costume—she was a brilliant actress. Her gait went from light and quick to slow and hesitant, leaning heavily on her sturdy walking stick. Her ballerina posture shifted to hunched-over shoulders and a neck that stuck forward a few inches too far. Only her eyes still spoke of the spirited, elegant woman I knew.

"Is this seat taken, dear?" Etta asked Principal Olivia Gibson tremulously.

"Gram, leave her alone, there's plenty of seats over here." I shot the principal an apologetic look while Etta sent her a forlorn one.

"No, that's okay," Gibson said, demonstrating she had a heart. "She can sit by me."

"Oh, that's real lovely of you." Etta teetered her way up onto the stool, making it look so difficult that I found myself ready to catch her. "My granddaughter here, she's always worried about being polite. But I'm more interested in meeting people. I count myself blessed if I get out once a week nowadays, and I need to feel involved in this world somehow. Hear people's stories. Otherwise, I sit around, feeling like the world's just waiting for me to pass on. You don't mind do you?"

"No." Principal Gibson took a large swig, suggesting she kind of did. "Not at all."

"Well. Let me buy you a drink then," Etta said. "Barman, another of what she's having please, and I'll have a scotch on the rocks. Izzy there'll have a club soda." She turned to Gibson and winked. "She's designated driver. There's gotta be some benefit to getting old."

I had the feeling Etta was enjoying this more than she should.

"Don't drink too much, Gram. You know what happened last week."

She flapped her hand at me. "Piffle. You just don't know what a good time looks like." She swiveled back to Gibson. "Now tell me. What do you do with yourself?"

"I'm a principal," she said.

"Get outta here. I used to be a teacher back in the day. What made you get into it?"

Another swig. "I've been asking myself the same question."

Etta chuckled appreciatively. "It's a thankless job, I'll bet. I always used to say, the kids were great, at least some of them were. But the paperwork was soul destroying. I imagine the principal gig is worse?"

"It can be. Though it's less the paperwork and more the politics that drives me to drink."

"I hear you. There's the schoolyard politics—a whole mini infrastructure of juvenile society—and then there's teacher and parent politics, which is about a hundred times as bad. Where are you principal of?"

"Frederick Academy."

"Now that's a school with some prestige behind it. Well done." She took a sip of her own drink. "But wait, isn't that the one in the news? With the parent murdered and some other parent arrested for it?"

"Now you know why I'm here instead of at home with my feet up. My holidays will be spent smoothing the feathers of overprotective parents and making bland, consolatory statements to the press."

"That bad, huh? At least they can't blame the school, right? It'd be quite another thing if a parent took out a teacher or vice versa. I've met a few parents I would've liked to take out, I can tell you that."

It was Gibson who chuckled appreciatively this time. Less heartily than Etta had, but she must have been warming to the conversation.

"Just a few?" she asked.

Etta snorted. "I wish you'd been the principal at my school. The guy was as sour as a gherkin and had no sense of humor at all. I guess I would've been sour too if my last name had been Goober. But I want to hear your story. What happened? What was the guy who was murdered like? Or what was his kid like? You can tell a lot about a parent by their kid."

"His kid's a wreck. You'd think it'd happen less at a highly regarded school full of rich kids, but sometimes I think it's worse. At the very least, they're as bad as the rest of us, only in shinier packaging."

"Did you see it coming? Was the father the kind to make enemies?"

"Well, he put on a good front, but I've been around long enough to see his real colors. Just before school finished for the winter holidays, he got into an all-out shouting match with the guy they're looking at for the murder. The victim's son was bullying the other guy's daughter. A learned behavior if you get my drift. That kid felt no qualms about beating someone up. And the girl's a smart one—earned herself a scholarship—but she seems to be born a victim. Always denies being beaten up, which means my hands are tied and I can't discipline the bully unless we catch him in the act. It's a total mess."

It was a total mess all right. Michael's son was bullying Joy? And Mr. Black had gotten into a shouting match with Mr. Watts over it a few days before Watts had been found shot in his home?

Mr. Black had promised me it was nothing personal. That it was a professional job. He'd lied through his giant teeth. Which meant he probably did it.

Maybe he'd gone to beat Michael up like his boss had instructed and gotten carried away. Or maybe his boss hadn't been lying when he denied sending him. Abraham Black was very protective of his daughter.

"Wait, you think the victim beat his son?" Etta said, and I was glad the onus was on her to carry the conversation while I was reeling. "Is that what you mean by learned behavior?"

"I tried calling child services, but you know how they are—they won't do anything unless the kid is almost dead. If then. And they're even worse with rich folk. So perhaps something good will come out of the whole thing. With the father gone the kid might learn how to be a functional member of society. His mom seems okay."

"Not so great for the other kid though if her daddy goes to jail for protecting her."

"Nah." Gibson tipped back the last of her drink. "She comes to school with all sorts of injuries too. That's what I meant when I said born to be a victim. Those kids are both stuck in nasty patterns of behavior, but with their fathers out of the picture, hopefully that pattern will break."

Crap. She obviously didn't know about Joy's parkour hobby. But I wasn't in a position to set her straight.

"Well, cheers to that," Etta said.

"Cheers to that," Principal Olivia Gibson repeated.

———

"WE NEED TO TALK TO MR. BLACK," I told Etta grimly. "Now."

I'd let her finish her drink, then reminded her it was time for her medication and made a show of escorting her to the car. As soon as we were back in our seats, I'd let the mask drop.

Etta shook her head in disappointment. "I suspected you'd feel that way."

Her tone implied she'd come to a different conclusion than I had about who our latest findings suggested was guilty. But she was determined to think of Mr. Black as innocent.

"If Principal Gibson has her facts straight, Michael's wife had a lot of motive," she pointed out. "Besides, they say it's almost always the spouse, don't they?"

"But she has an alibi."

"Well, so do most people who have time to plan a murder."

It was a fair point, but she could have also had an alibi because she was innocent. Mr. Black had mentioned he'd made sure no one else was home.

"I don't know," I said. "If he abused his kid for years and possibly her too, what changed?"

"Maybe she snapped. Hell, I'd kill the bastard in her shoes."

"That's just it. In her shoes, you'd never have put up with that for a minute, let alone years."

"Hmm, you're right about that. I would've dragged his sorry ass to a tattoo parlor and gotten 'LOSER' tattooed across his forehead, then left him in a swamp in Louisiana for an alligator to eat."

I was momentarily sidetracked by that image.

"And if she did snap, then I guess she wouldn't have had the chance to plan an alibi," Etta admitted.

"I don't feel comfortable trying to pin this on her without solid evidence. She's grieving, and it sounds like she has a lot to process."

"Yet you're A-okay with it being pinned on Abe without solid evidence."

Ever the diplomat, I didn't point out that there was plenty of solid evidence, and it all implicated Mr. Black. "I'm helping, aren't I?"

"Sure, but I saw that look in your eyes. Now you heard about that bullying thing, you think he did it again."

My first instinct was to deny it, but I exhaled instead. "It's true. But I'm really hoping I'm wrong."

There was no point arguing anymore about it until we'd heard what he had to say, so I changed the topic. "Were you ever actually a teacher?"

"Hell no, didn't have the patience for it. But I had friends who were—enough to know what they liked to complain about. Quickest way to mutual ground is having a common enemy."

"Or a common appreciation," I said, thinking of the first time we'd met. "Like cookies."

"Cookies and Connor," Etta corrected me. She'd appreciated the eye candy Connor had provided at least as much as the cookies.

I wondered whether I could use either concept to befriend Emily. Unfortunately, the one thing we seemed to have in common was the job she was determined to beat me at. Oh, and our mutual dislike of each other. Nope, I'd have to go with plan A.

Etta fixed her lipstick, removed the coke-bottle glasses, and left the walking stick in the car. There was nothing she could do about her clothes.

The Black family was too polite to comment on her change of attire. We gathered around the dining table like the first time I'd met Hallie and Joy. It was a lot more crowded with Abraham's bulk added to the group.

"You need to tell us the truth," I said to him. "We know how protective you are of Joy." It was hard to say the words with her sitting right there, but we had to get to the bottom of this, and it was her parents' decision to involve her, not mine. "What happened? Did Watts fight back? Did he threaten her?"

"No, nothing like that. I didn't do it." His voice was pleading. "I avoided mentioning the bullying thing because I know how it looks, and Joy told me how hard it was to convince you to help."

Great, so now it was my fault.

Judging by my guilt levels, part of me agreed with him. The other part of me was convinced he'd done it and was stringing me along in an effort to get free. Although why he thought I could help, I'd never know. Etta must have greatly overexaggerated my skill set and connections.

"I'll admit it. I kind of enjoyed beating him up for Joy's sake." Mr. Black glanced at his daughter. "Sorry, honey, but I did." He rubbed a hand over his head as he often did when he was agitated or deep in thought. "If I'd been more sensible, I might have asked for a different assignment, but I figured the bastard would be too proud to tell anyone what happened and that it might teach him a lesson."

He absentmindedly slipped a dollar bill into the battered pig on the table. The swear jar, I remembered.

"But Watts was alive when I left. Honest. And I'm sorry. I should've told you anyway, but I was scared you wouldn't help, and then I'd have to leave Joy and Hallie."

His daughter shifted in her chair. "Why are you so quick to think Dad did it? The victim was an asshole!"

"Joy!" Hallie admonished.

"What? It's true. You know he beat up his son? Where do you think his son learned to be a nasty-ass bully from, huh? I bet there were loads of people who wanted him dead."

"Swear jar. Now."

"Principal Gibson did insinuate that Michael beat up his son," Etta said thoughtfully. "But then it kind of sounded like she thought Abe beat you up as well, Joy. Probably because of your parkour injuries."

Joy turned white. "Sorry, Dad. I never thought—"

"It's fine, love. What the principal thinks is the least of our problems."

"I guess so. But next time she asks me about how I got an injury, I'll tell her the truth. I've always avoided it in case she thought it seemed dumb or uncouth or something. But I'd prefer she think I'm a silly little girl than think you . . . well, you know. You're an awesome father, and I love you." She wrapped her spindly arms around his giant trunk of a waist.

I noticed through blurry eyes that her arms couldn't reach all the way around.

But it didn't put my fear that Mr. Black killed Michael to rest. It was because he was such a great father that made me think he might have.

12

IN THE MOVIES, surveillance is exciting. The surveillance partners sit in the car, and then the scene cuts to the person they're spying on doing something that initiates an action sequence. On the few occasions the sitting in the car scene goes longer, the partners have snacks and deep and meaningful conversations.

Etta and I had run out of both snacks and deep and meaningful conversation, and our target had yet to leave the house. We'd been sitting here for five hours. The car was cold without the engine and heater running. I had a recurring cramp in my left butt cheek, and Etta needed to pee.

"Seriously," I said, "even if she did murder her husband, what would she possibly get up to almost a week later that would help us prove she did it?"

Etta sat with her legs crossed to convince her bladder to wait a while longer and pursed her lips. "I don't know. Maybe she's got a boyfriend who's about to drop around. Maybe she needs to find a better hiding place for the murder weapon. Maybe she'll start a fire in the backyard, burn their wedding photos, and urinate on the ashes."

"Got peeing on the brain, do you?"

"Shut up." She crossed her legs tighter.

I smirked before the evil butt cramp struck again. Then it was Etta's turn to smirk as I twisted and contorted in the tight confines of my Corvette to ease it.

"All right," she said a while later. "We'll give it ten more minutes, then we'll go have lunch and a bathroom break."

I was trying to come up with a way of suggesting we not come back. Or that we at least come back in separate shifts to halve the amount of time I'd waste, when a black sedan parked across the street. A handsome man got out.

"Ha. I told you she had a boyfriend!" Etta crowed.

A second man exited the vehicle. This one had a remarkably round head with just a tuft of hair on top. It reminded me of an onion. "Not unless she's into threesomes."

"Could be."

Onion Head opened the trunk and grabbed a leather tool roll.

"Kinky threesomes with tools," I amended.

"Well her husband was into weird stuff. She might be too."

I shook my head. "The earth must be a more interesting place in your mind than mine."

"Undoubtedly."

I resisted enquiring how come she was bored so often then.

See? Always diplomatic.

The men had walked up to the front door, their broad backs blocking our view of Nicole's face, and disappeared inside.

"Come on," Etta said. "We need to get closer."

My desire to stretch my aching butt fought with my desire to stay safe. My aching butt won. I didn't want to consider what that said about me.

We walked casually to the neighboring home and ducked down behind the hedge that divided the two properties. If Etta was hoping we'd be able to see through it, her hopes were about to be dashed. It was thick, healthy foliage two feet wide. I was just hoping the Watts' neighbors weren't home. We'd seen two cars leave this morning, but it was no guarantee the house was empty.

"Now what?" I hissed.

Music started blaring from the Watts' residence. Stealers Wheel "Stuck in the Middle with You." Too loud for normal conversation inside and too loud for this quiet residential street.

"I don't think they're having a dance party," Etta said.

"Nobody would want to dance to that garbage. We need to risk getting closer." She prodded the hedge experimentally. "I'm going around."

Returning the way we came, we saw that the front curtains on the left side of the house had been drawn. What the heck was going on? Had Etta been right about the weird sex thing?

Weird loud sex might explain the music.

Since the privacy afforded by the curtains went both ways, we figured it was safe to approach. We crossed the garden and slipped down the left side of the house. The curtains facing the neighboring hedge were still open. I guess Mrs. Watts knew exactly how spy-proof that foliage was. We crouched underneath the window and tried to hear anything past the music.

Someone screamed.

Etta risked poking her head past the windowsill for half a second. "She's tied up. There's blood. Those rotten bastards are torturing her." She met my gaze, her eyes steely. "Have you got your pepper spray?"

I patted my pocket. These days, I usually kept it in my bag, but I'd put it in my pocket in honor of our surveillance—before I'd learned how boring the reality version was. Or had been. But my pocket was empty. "Damn! It must've fallen out in the car when I was stretching to get the cramp out."

Etta rolled her eyes. "Well for goodness' sake. Run back and get it, then go and ring the doorbell. We'll divide and conquer. You take out whoever answers the door, and I'll deal with whoever stays here."

"What about the police?"

"I'll call them while you're getting the pepper spray, but they'll take too long to get here. Do you really want to sit and do nothing while she's tortured?"

Another scream tore through the music and galvanized me into action. I sprinted for the car. Found the pepper spray in the footwell under a crisps packet. Raced to the front door. Readied the safety tab on the spray before tucking it behind me and rang the doorbell. My heart drummed in my chest. What if they didn't bother to come? What if they both came? What if—

Handsome opened the door with a friendly smile. "Hey, girl. What can I do for you?"

Crap. I was too close. Close enough that he might disarm me before I had a chance to aim. "Um." I looked down, as if shy, and took a step back. Then I whipped the canister out and started spraying. In my terror, I depressed the nozzle too soon and sprayed a foot of the wall before any of it hit his face. But at least it hit his face.

He cursed and spluttered and made a blind grab for me. I fled around the side of the house. Maybe my sub-conscious wanted to give Etta backup, or maybe I was running to her for protection. She was the one with the Glock, after all. I heard a shot as I ran and the shattering of glass. By the time I reached the window, it was gone and so was Etta.

I peeked over the sill. Etta was standing over Mrs. Watts, her Glock angled at the nearest doorway. The black sedan burned rubber as it took off up the street. I hoisted myself gingerly through the window and switched off the blasted music. Nicole Watts was crying, and two of her toenails were missing. The sight turned my stomach and made me wish that I'd had something more damaging than pepper spray on hand.

"They're gone now," I said. "It's going to be okay."

With the music off, I could hear the wailing of sirens in the distance. Police and an ambulance. Etta and I started working on the ropes that bound Nicole.

"Th-thank you." She wept.

In the face of her distress, it didn't seem right to ask the questions gnawing at us. Who were those men? What did they want? Could they have killed her husband?

As the last of the authorities drove away, Etta crossed her arms. "Well, hell. All of that and we still didn't find out anything concrete to help Abe."

13

CONNOR HADN'T REACHED out since our conversation about him needing to open up yesterday. Not a phone call, message, or suggestion of a time to catch up. While my instinct was to seek him out and try to work things through, possibly to the point of rocking up on his doorstep, I'd decided to give him space.

From my observations and what Harper had said, this was a big step for him. I'd told him how important this was to me. For us. Now he needed to think it over and come to his own conclusion.

You can't force someone to be vulnerable, to bare their soul, to trust. So if Connor didn't choose to open up, that was that. I couldn't do anything about it. My lungs constricted at the thought.

The one positive from this whole crappy situation was that I still hadn't had the opportunity to tell Connor about taking on Mr. Black's case. Even apart from the fact that I wasn't looking forward to breaking the news, I was starting to think it was a good thing. Showing him what it was like to be in my shoes in this relationship could be a useful illustration. A convincing one.

He'd be furious about it. Especially given the danger of this afternoon's events. But perhaps he needed to be furious to take the two-way communication thing seriously.

Yep. It was for the best, I decided as I stuck a Band-Aid over a cut I'd gotten climbing through the broken window.

But I missed him. All of me missed him.

———

ON THE SUBJECT OF TEACHING people lessons, I was almost looking forward to giving Emily a taste of her own medicine. Maybe she'd realize how petty she was being and call a truce.

And maybe my ex-husband could fly.

Vanessa had informed me that this evening would be a "friendly" social gathering of eight of the WECS Club women. In other words, poison would be as common as table salt. Of course, I'd banned Vanessa from using the table salt in case it had been spiked.

My bag was fuller than usual as I made the trek from the parking lot. I'd brought along a few accessories, as well as a tote bag scrunched up down the bottom to hide everything in once I reached the storage closet—to make it harder for Emily to tamper with my stuff. If I'd been clever enough to set up some kind of booby trap, I would've done that instead. Perhaps I'd Google it later.

I slipped a carefully chosen bottle into my pocket. Its contents weren't going to be ingested, and they weren't going to hurt anyone. They were just going to teach Emily Lin that I wasn't the doormat she thought I was.

I put my handbag into the tote bag and shoved them into the back of a cubbyhole I hadn't used before. It wouldn't stand up to a thorough search, but hopefully if she went to the trouble of finding it, someone would spot her rummaging through everyone's bags.

Vanessa and her merry band of backstabbing conspirers were in full swing. Didn't they have anything better to do with their lives? I supposed the answer must have been no, or they wouldn't have joined the WECS Club in the first place.

The current topic of conversation was advice for Stephanie and her unborn child.

"Whatever you do, don't breastfeed, darling, or those assets of yours will depreciate faster than you'd believe possible."

"Nonsense, she can breastfeed if she wants. I can't imagine why anyone would, but we all know you can get those assets perked up with the help of a good surgeon. It's the natural birth you need to avoid at all costs. That particular asset is harder to fix."

Stephanie's naturally wide-eyed look was teetering toward bug-eyed. Two of the talkers exchanged a smirk.

I'd been wondering how Stephanie had gotten into the inner circle of the club members. She didn't seem to have the sophisticated cruelty the others had perfected. Now I had my answer. They'd let her in for sport.

"Have you looked into potential night nurses yet? The good ones need to be headhunted in advance, or you don't know what kind of creature you'll end up with. They might steal your valuables."

"Or your husband," another woman chimed in.

"And make sure you put your child on the Frederick Academy waiting list as soon as you decide on a name."

I swooped in to save Vanessa from a dose of laxatives in her celery root soup appetizer that would have seen her keeping an all-night vigil on the porcelain throne. Then I tuned them out. These were not people I wanted to take advice from.

Forty minutes later, the moment I'd been waiting for arrived. Emily and I went downstairs at the same time. My chance to get even.

I patted the pocket containing the bottle and suppressed my glee so it wouldn't give me away. While she went into the kitchen, forcing me to wait outside, I would put my plan into action.

However, when she swung open the kitchen door, instead of disappearing inside, she halted. From where I was standing, I could see her profile. She was holding on to the doorframe, as if to steady herself, and swallowed hard.

"Are you okay?" I asked, not sure what I wanted her answer to be.

"Fine," she said.

Perspiration beaded on her upper lip, and she wiped it away.

Oh great, just when I was finally going to get her back, she fell ill. "Was something you tasted poisoned?" I tried again.

She gave a sharp nod. "I'm fine, only nauseous. I was okay until I smelled all this food cooking."

If she couldn't bear to smell it, how was she going to taste it? A large part of me wanted to smile and suggest she try the tempura eel. Maybe I should. She'd given me every reason to. But as I watched her throat bob again, trying to keep back the rising gorge, I knew I couldn't do it. I was a sucker that way. Blame my endlessly kindhearted mother.

Dammit. I was looking forward to seeing her hands glued to a plate.

"All right. I think we got off on the wrong foot," I said. "But I'd like to help you. Can we start over?"

She was staring at the pots and pans of food in the kitchen as if they were a pack of zombies getting ready to swarm, putrid flesh hanging from their bones. Maybe she hadn't heard me.

I pulled her away from the door. "You need to get out of there. Tell me what you want, and I'll taste it for you."

Her distrust of me warred with necessity. "Miranda can have whatever Vanessa's having," she bit out, then retreated from the hall.

When someone eventually came out to take my order, I requested the geranium and Meyer lemon gelato with crumble. It was an almost carnal pleasure to sample them both. Patching up the presentation was more of a chore, but I managed that too.

Emily was standing outside, where I'd escaped to the first night, drawing in lungfuls of air. She looked a bit better for it. I offered her a plate.

"Give me the other one," she said. Her tone was a challenge. As if she genuinely thought I might have poisoned it.

It was a line even she hadn't crossed. Probably for no reason other than the Taste Society would boot her out if she did.

I gave her the one she requested, and we climbed up the stairs, served our clients, and returned to our stations.

For a moment there, I'd hoped it might be a chance for a new start between us, but she refused to meet my gaze for the next hour.

Pity. It would have been nice to have someone to share a laugh at this alien world with.

The WECS Club women stopped their posturing an hour later and departed at the same time. On the way out of the clubhouse, Emily shouldered past me and spoke in a low undertone. "Thanks. For helping me."

I watched her black ponytail swing with each step and wondered if I might get that new start after all.

———

MY DEEP SLEEP WAS BROKEN by the sound of glass shattering and a thump. At first I thought I must be dreaming of our rescue of Nicole Watts. Then more glass shattered and I heard the sudden whoosh of flames.

Crap.

I fumbled for the lamp switch and leaped out of bed. Meow lifted her head to watch me. I raced out into the living area, slamming the door behind me when I caught sight of the flames licking the dining table and the nearby sofa.

Black, dirty smoke was already clouding the air. For a split second I was torn between grabbing Meow and fleeing or grabbing the fire extinguisher and trying to put it out.

My lack of insurance made me lunge for the extinguisher. Why the hell had I never learned to use one of these things? I squinted at the instruction pictures, feeling like an idiot, then released the pin and pointed the hose at the flames. I couldn't believe how quickly it was spreading.

The fire alarm finally started shrieking as the smoke wafted toward the kitchen. "Very helpful," I muttered and then regretted it when I inhaled a lungful of smoke and chemical powder from the extinguisher. Coughing and spluttering, I focused on the kitchen side of the flames, wanting to keep my pathway to the one exit clear.

Somebody pounded on the door, but since it would take me precious seconds to dart over there and open the deadbolt and chain, I ignored it. More glass shattered. I ducked and shielded my head instinctively, as if that would help me against another firebomb. Then a second stream of extinguisher powder spurted through the window. I could just make out Etta's white hair through the darkness and smoke.

That was much more helpful.

Tense seconds later, the flames were out. I went to the door, stepping around the smoldering carcass of the dining table, and joined Etta on the gloriously less smoky stair landing.

"Thanks," I said, then started another coughing fit.

She patted me on the back, which didn't help but was somehow comforting all the same. "No problem, dear. You know how I hate it when you have too much excitement without me. What in the name of George Clooney happened here?"

"I don't know. I was in bed when I heard glass smashing, and then the flames started and everything was burning. I think it might've been one of those Molotov cocktail thingies." I eyed the smoke billowing out the open doorway and watched it drift up to join the smog that formed a canopy over LA. "Let me go check on Meow."

My bedroom was relatively smoke-free, and Meow hadn't moved from her favorite spot on my pillow. Though judging by the angle of her ears, she didn't appreciate the shrieking smoke alarm. I opened the window to let some fresh air in and resisted the urge to pick her up. I reeked a lot worse than my room did, and she might not appreciate that any more than the smoke alarm. My phone was buzzing on my bedside table. Connor.

So now he wants to talk.

No doubt his security team had reported strange activity from my surveillance camera. I grabbed the phone but didn't answer it. Content Meow was safe, I shut her in again, then opened all the other windows in the apartment and put the fan on in an effort to shut the damn alarm up.

By the time I made it back outside, my neighbors from the whole apartment building had come out to see what the fuss was about.

Ms. Pleasant, the least pleasant person in the building, had her hair in rollers and was clutching a purple bathrobe around her like one of the other neighbors might try to rip it off. Her efforts were wasted. I couldn't imagine anyone wanting to ogle her in her nightclothes.

"What's going on here?" she asked peevishly. "Don't you know some people need to sleep?"

The Flanagans were huddled together—Mrs. Flanagan in a sexy nightie and Mr. Flanagan in boxers and a T-shirt. Based on their proximity, they must have been in a fornicating rather than fighting phase at the moment.

Mr. Larson was standing in shorts and bare feet, a hamster cage tucked under his arm and a gun tucked into his waistband. As a former military man, he had prepared to fight or evacuate. I liked him more for the fact that he'd deemed only his hamster worth saving in the event of an evacuation.

Mr. Winkle was in plaid pajamas and empty-handed. If there'd been an emergency, his prized fighting fish would've had to fend for themselves. But to be fair, fish didn't take kindly to being transported.

Only the young Koreans hadn't bothered to come out and see what was happening. If Etta's updates were to be believed, they might not have heard the fire alarm over their video game headsets, or they'd been too high to care.

"Uh, sorry everyone," I called out, my voice rough from the smoke. "There was a small fire in my apartment, but it's been put out now and you can all go back to sleep."

Mutters. Glares. Sympathy. One by one, they shuffled inside, and a moment later Connor's car slammed to a stop on the road below. Oops. Out of the fire into the . . . well something bad. I'd meant to call him back as soon as I'd gotten the alarm to shut up.

We watched Connor stride up the stairs. Etta with pure appreciation. Me with a combination of comfort and dread. I didn't know how it was possible for someone to make me feel so safe and nervous at the same time.

He stormed across the landing, his jaw tight and eyes hard, and wrapped me in a hug.

"Now you're going to smell as bad as me," I told him after we'd stood entwined for a minute. Despite the disaster of the fire, his vicinity was melting away my valid concerns from the last few days and putting impractical ideas in my head.

The bedroom was hardly even damaged, my newly awakened beast pointed out. Nothing impractical about it.

"Then we'll both need a shower," Connor said, still pressed against me. Suddenly there was more of him pressed against me.

"The bathroom escaped the worst of the fire," I found myself volunteering before I could think better of it.

All humor drained from his voice. "Tell me what happened."

14

"IT'S A LONG STORY, and we're both tired," I hedged. "Can we sleep it off and talk about it in the morning?"

Maybe Connor would react better after a few extra hours sleep and a big breakfast.

He gave me a look that suggested he knew exactly what I was up to. Then he stepped inside and surveyed the smoking wreckage that had once been my humble apartment. "Do you have renters insurance?"

I shook my head, and his jaw tightened some more.

"Why the hell not? You can get it for as little as one hundred and fifty bucks a year."

"That's very helpful, thanks."

It kind of was actually. I would never have guessed renters insurance was so cheap. But when I'd moved in a mere four months ago, I hadn't had anywhere close to one hundred fifty bucks to spare, and I didn't appreciate being scolded right now.

If I was lucky, Oliver might have insurance. I owned almost nothing anyway.

Connor was crouching over something. "My security guys told me two masked men came and smashed the window, then threw a Molotov cocktail inside." The grim set to his mouth promised he was going to question me extensively about that later. "You'll need to file a police report. There's glass from the bottle here, and I'll prep the video footage for you as well."

"Okay." I hadn't had the chance to think that far ahead, and the reminder of all the mundane practicalities to come depleted the last of my adrenaline. What I'd said to Connor was true; I was exhausted. As much emotionally as physically. Maybe it was the residual smoke making the room move around me, but I felt like I was swaying on my feet.

Connor came over to my side and steadied me. "Sorry." The word was soft and probably hard for him to say. "We can deal with all that after you've had some sleep. You can stay at my place while it gets sorted out. Meow too."

"Thank you."

"Don't worry about packing now. We'll come here in the morning. But the chemicals in the extinguisher will eat through softer materials if we leave them covered in it. Is there anything worth saving?"

I glanced around, doing a quick mental inventory.

"Nope."

"Then let's go."

"What about Etta and my other neighbors? What if those men come back?"

"Well, I guess I have enough rooms for everyone at my place."

It took me longer than it should have to process the words and realize he was making a joke, trying to cheer me up.

He didn't wait for me to catch on. "I'll have one of my security personnel watch the building for the rest of the night."

"Thank you," I said again. Then I collected Meow, apologizing since I stank enough that she'd need a bath later, hugged and thanked Etta for helping me, and followed Connor to his car. I was grateful the seats were odor-resistant leather.

It was four a.m. when we arrived at Connor's home in Beverly Hills. Meow wound herself once around my legs and then trotted off to explore. "Don't get lost," I called after her. "This place is friggin' huge." Especially for a cat who'd spent most of her life in a tiny apartment. I'd have to find her before I fell into bed and make sure she knew where her water and makeshift cat litter was. Otherwise, the lie I'd once told Mr. Black about her pooping in shoes might come true.

I turned to Connor. "I'm going to shower."

His gaze heated. "Do you want company?"

"With your mom here? No way!"

"If that's your only protest, remember what you just finished telling Meow: This place is friggin' huge."

I shook my head and entered the bathroom. "We'll continue this debate some other time." A moment later, I stuck my head out. "Oh, and I um, might need to use that spare set of pajamas and undies Maria bought for me."

Connor smirked. "Coming right up."

I climbed back into bed—this time beside Connor who was already clean and asleep—at four thirty. The shower had woken me up a little, and my mind had started fretting over bringing him up to speed on all my escapades of the last few days. That and the minor problem of having to deal with the police, landlord, repairs, and the reality that someone had set my apartment on fire. With me inside.

Every time I began drifting closer to sleep, my brain would conjure the sound of crashing glass or the sight of flames and I'd be jolted awake again. I switched on the bedside lamp, planning on waking Connor up and telling him I'd changed my mind about waiting until morning to go over everything. I wanted to see the video footage for myself.

But even in the low light, I could see that the toll his mom's health scare and now my burning apartment had taken on him. Besides, he looked so peaceful. I left him there and sought out Meow.

She'd finished exploring, and I found her in the laundry of all places, curled up on a clean pile of washing. "Seriously? You have at least a dozen rooms of soft spots to choose from and you end up here?" Maybe she was feeling overwhelmed by the size of the place and so had chosen the smallest room she could find. It was also where I'd put her water and makeshift litter box.

I picked her up, noticing the acrid scent of smoke on her coat now that I'd washed it off myself, and carried her to bed. She magnanimously accepted her relocation and settled in between Connor and me. After that, I managed to fall asleep.

———

MORNING SUN FILTERED THROUGH the paned window, giving me a gorgeous view of the bare limbs of the oak trees against a clear blue sky outside. Connor was gone, and Meow was curled up on his pillow. The sight made me smile. Then I remembered why we were both here rather than at home in our humble apartment.

On the bright side. Here had espresso coffee.

Instead of finding Maria in the kitchen—whose official title was maid but whose job description was Connor's right-hand woman—I found Connor's mom Mae. She was an intelligent, plucky woman who'd worked as a private investigator and single-handedly raised two kids after her military husband was killed in action. Now retired, she tended her garden, excelled at crosswords, distilled her own gin, and—if Harper's warning was to be believed—did occasional surveillance on her adult children's new friends, bosses, or lovers.

Mae pulled me into a warm hug. We'd met each other less than a week ago, but we'd instantly hit it off.

Well, not quite instantly. The first words out of her mouth had me ready to flee the eighty-four miles back to Palms until I'd realized it was a prank. Oh, and then I'd had to ruin Christmas lunch to secretly stop her from being poisoned.

But we'd really gotten along for the time in the interim.

Lucky she was the forgiving sort.

"Connor told me about last night, you poor thing," she said. "Are you all right?"

"Yes, thanks, I'm okay. I was about to ask you the same question." I wasn't the one who'd been in hospital recently.

She patted my cheek. "One hundred and ten percent. Connor's just fussier than an old mother hen."

I laughed at the image she painted and hoped that his fussing would make it difficult for her to put me under surveillance. But at least if she did, my current Shade assignment looked innocuous enough from the outside.

"I guess he is," I agreed. "Though he'd never admit it. Can I help you with those eggs? Where's Maria?"

"No need, I have it covered. I made Connor give Maria the week off. If he's going to force me to stay here when"— she raised her voice so Connor, who must've been in the dining room, could hear—"I'm perfectly fine, then the least I could do was make myself useful. But you might want to prepare your own coffee. Connor said you're even more particular than he is."

"I'm afraid he's right. Can I make you one while I'm at it?"

"Sadly no. I can't drink coffee this early in the morning anymore. Makes me jittery. Especially that espresso kind which tends to pack more of a punch than the filter. I used to live off the stuff when I was running our PI business and raising Connor and Harper. But that's what getting old does to you." She flipped the contents of the pan with an energy that belied her getting-old comment.

"My neighbor's in her seventies and doesn't consider herself old. You've got a way to go yet."

She huffed. "Tell that to Connor, will you? Every year he treats me like I'm more and more breakable. It's enough to give me a complex."

"I think he treats everyone he cares about that way," I muttered, thinking of the news I still hadn't told him. Meow interrupted our conversation by trotting into the kitchen and loudly announcing it was breakfast time. "Mae, meet Meow, my housemate's cat. She must've heard us talking about food." Except I didn't think to bring anything for her from the apartment.

Mae read my mind. "We don't have any cat food here, but we have leftover roast lamb."

Meow meowed her approval.

"She loves roast lamb," I translated. "But what about Agatha? Is she here too?" Agatha was Mae's German short-haired pointer. Named in honor of Agatha Christie, though this Agatha preferred chewing books to writing them.

"A friend of mine's looking after her back home. She's used to running around off leash and swimming in the pond, so it's hard to give her enough exercise in the city."

Probably just as well. Meow took a long time to warm up to Dudley. We left her eating her gourmet breakfast and joined Connor in the dining room with coffee, eggs, bacon, mushrooms, spinach, and tomato.

"How did you sleep?" he asked me. His jaw was freshly shaven and his hair damp from the shower. My appetite shifted from a desire for food to a different sort of hankering.

"Before or after the fire?" I joked.

He didn't look amused. "About that. Want to tell me why someone would toss a Molotov cocktail through your window?"

The moment of truth. Except with his mom here I couldn't even use the lines I'd prepared when I'd last met him for breakfast. "Um. Can I see that video footage first?"

After a long look at me, he tapped his tablet a couple of times and we all huddled around to watch. The recording from the security camera on my front door was grainy but showed enough detail. Two men in masks that looked like they'd been left over from Halloween entered the screen. One was tall and muscular, the other short and stocky with a familiar tuft of hair on top of his head.

"Guess I should have sprayed Handsome before he could get a proper look at me," I mused, wondering how they'd found my apartment.

Connor shifted one eyebrow. "Handsome?"

"I nicknamed him before the whole firebombing thing."

"Oh. That's okay then."

I nodded absentmindedly, still trying to figure out why they'd found my apartment and not Etta's.

"You've got some explaining to do," Connor growled.

"Uh, right."

I looked from one face to the other. Mae's was pleasant and interested, Connor's a stony mask. I took a swig of my espresso to fortify myself and bravely launched into the whole sorry tale.

Connor exploded when I detailed our rescue of the widow. "What the hell were you thinking?"

"Of stopping Nicole from being tortured?"

"You should've left it to the police. What if they'd decided to shoot back?"

"Etta's probably a better shot, and I ran away very fast, like you taught me." He scowled at the reminder that he'd been the one to equip me with the pepper spray in the first place. "Besides, who knows what they would've done to Nicole in the time it had taken the police to arrive, assess the situation, and act."

"I'm sure she appreciated your quick thinking and courage," Mae said, earning another scowl from Connor. "Is there anything I can do to help with the case?"

"Mom, don't get involved, and for heaven's sake don't encourage her."

"Nonsense, hon, you're too protective for your own good. I know it's hard to deal with after what happened with your dad, but stopping your loved ones from living out of your fear of losing them isn't love. You have to find a way of giving them their freedom and being okay with that somehow. Besides, I need something to keep my mind occupied since you've got me stuck here away from my projects."

Connor hung his head in his hands. The largest gesture of defeat I'd ever seen from him. But when he lifted it again, his expression was resolute. He looked my way. "We'll talk about you getting involved in a case I told you absolutely not to later. Right now we need to track down the bastards that did this and make sure they don't get the chance to try again."

It sounded like a good plan to me. With any luck, we'd be tracking down Michael Watts's murderer at the same time. Those thugs had certainly proven they had no aversion to violence.

15

CONNOR PUSHED back from the table and strode out of the dining room, mumbling something about clearing his schedule for the day. Mae and I lingered over our breakfasts.

"Best to give him space to compose himself," she said.

We chatted about where I might find affordable furniture to replace what had been lost, and Mae offered to help with all the washing and cleaning. An offer that brought tears to my eyes. It was the kind of thing my mum would have volunteered to do, had she been here, and I felt a pang of homesickness as well as a wave of gratitude at Mae's kindness.

Meow was less grateful since she was first on the cleaning agenda.

When Connor didn't return, I left to prepare myself for the day. He came into the en-suite when I was brushing my teeth.

"I've been thinking about what you said," he told me. "About sharing stuff with you, I mean."

Nice of him to start this conversation when I couldn't talk back. I braced myself for the "and I've decided you're an idiot" conclusion. I wouldn't give up on him. Not yet. But I didn't know how to get through to him either.

"It's hard to wrap my mind around your point of view when I've been living the way I have for so long," he said instead.

That wasn't what I was expecting to hear. That sounded like he might be willing to budge.

His hand rested on the door like he wanted to keep his exit clear, and his eyes studied the tiles. I suspected he'd prefer to be facing the barrel of a gun than having this conversation. "When your work is classified," he went on, "the less information you give, the fewer lies you need to remember. So it's easier to stop talking . . . And once you stop talking, it's easier to stop caring."

He met my gaze in the mirror.

"That's why you were such a pain in the ass. Not only did you force me to talk all the time, but you challenged me to care. To reassess my view of people. To reassess who I'd become." He swallowed as if the words were trying to crawl back down his throat before he could get them out.

"You have this frank, optimistic way of looking at the world. Even after what your ex did to you. You saw the Disney Princess watch on the guy coming to beat you up and asked about his family. You kept the damn turkey feather Dana's mom gave you even though you hate turkeys. You cared so much about your last client that you risked jail to track down his murderer. Somehow you manage to find the humor and humanity in any situation life throws at you. The world's a better place when I catch a glimpse of it through your eyes."

I spat into the sink. Unable to concentrate on brushing my teeth anymore.

He let go of the door to stand up straight and stiff. Like a soldier facing death. "I'm starting to see that if I want to be part of that world, I'm going to have to change some things. You deserve someone who makes you happy, and if that means talking and shit, then I'll try. But you're going to have to be patient with me."

I finished rinsing my mouth and went to him, no longer caring if his mom was in the same house. Funnily enough, I had no words to say. We were on the bed moments later. His need colliding with mine.

Meow had returned to her new favorite spot on Connor's pillow. For a second I felt weird about it. Then I forgot all about Meow.

———

CONNOR DROVE ME to the police station to file the report. I must have met my quota of misfortune for a while because I didn't run into Commander Hunt. Then we drove to my apartment to do a stocktake, pick up some clothes, and tell Etta the plan—or what we had of it anyway.

I surveyed the damage with fresh eyes: the cold, charred remains of what had once been our dining and living area. The stench of acrid smoke hit me anew, and I concluded reluctantly every single thing in the apartment would need to be washed to get the smell out.

The timber dining table had gone first, with one side completely burned to ash. It had toppled over when the two legs on the burned side no longer had a tabletop to attach to. The fabric couch that we'd managed to squeeze three people plus Dudley and Meow on was reduced to an ugly metal frame and one blackened armrest. One of the armchairs had fared better but would still have to be replaced thanks to the holes created by sparks. Piles of chemical powder coated every surface.

The single piece of good news was that the 1960s pineapple, banana, and flower wallpaper would finally have to go. I wondered whether Oliver would be disappointed after all his hard work at drawing eyes on the pineapples . . .

In that split second, I'd chosen to stay and fight because I didn't have insurance. But in the end, the only thing I'd managed to save was the stuff in our bedrooms and kitchen—after it'd been thoroughly cleaned. Then again, my neighbors probably appreciated not having their homes burned down.

Yes. I'd made the right decision. And I was lucky that with my new job as a Shade, having to fork out for a whole lot of budget or secondhand furniture and appliances wouldn't stop me from meeting my minimum repayments to the loan shark. Four months ago, this would have spelled the end.

But even apart from the money, I was dreading doing the mammoth amounts of cleaning and shopping required to put it back together again.

To my relief, Connor had told me the landlord would be responsible for replacing the carpet and fixing the smoke damage to the walls and ceiling. It was how it would've worked in Australia, but that's the thing about moving to a new country; all the laws and regulations that you learn growing up might be completely different. So I hadn't been sure until he'd said so.

I hoped the landlord would choose a carpet color other than sickly green. But maybe she liked it. Or maybe she'd get the exact same hue to spite us.

Unable to figure out where to begin, I wandered aimlessly to my bedroom and opened the door. The first thing I saw was my horrible rainbow-vomit duvet cover. Unlike the carpet, the stupid thing was untouched. Well, nothing that putting it through the wash wouldn't fix. I gently banged my head on the doorframe. "Looks like you and I are going to be together for a while longer yet."

"Were you talking to yourself?"

Connor's voice startled me. I'd left him in the car to make a phone call and hadn't heard him come in.

"Studies have shown that talking to yourself is actually beneficial," I informed him. "Albert Einstein talked to himself."

"You can be a genius if you want, honey. Your hair's crazy enough for it although it's the wrong color." He tugged a wayward red-brown lock to illustrate his point. "But I'd prefer it if you didn't adopt Einstein's mustache."

"Your preferences are noted. But I'm not making any promises."

He pulled me toward him and kissed me thoroughly. "I'll make it worth your while to stay mustache-free."

I laughed and pushed him away. But the silly conversation had lightened my mood and given me the wherewithal to collect the things I'd come for.

I selected a bunch of outfits appropriate for both WECS Club and sleuthing and put them in a suitcase along with my makeup and toiletries, phone charger, Taser, and my backup canister of pepper spray. I also made sure to pack Meow's food and litter box, though I suspected that with Mae around she'd be getting plenty of supplemental roast.

Etta let herself in. Apparently, with a gaping hole in the window and burned furniture, no one felt the need to knock anymore. She eyed my suitcase and Connor standing by.

"Jeepers. If I realized all it would take for you two to move in together was a little house fire, I would've set it up ages ago."

While Connor and I had only been dating a week, we'd told everyone we were in a relationship when we met in September. Connor had been my Taste Society client, and that had been the cover story we'd used to explain my spending every waking hour with him, sharing his food. Etta had been trying to get us back together ever since we'd "broken up." Probably because she liked having him around as eye candy.

"We both know you'd miss me too much if I moved out," I told her. She pursed her lips, so I figured I must be right. "The good news is, we've learned who did set the fire, and we need your help to stop them doing it again."

Etta grinned.

16

I BLEW FIFTY BUCKS on a bunch of flowers for Nicole and hated that I did it grudgingly. It was hard not to think about how much of a new dining table that could buy. But the poor woman had been tortured and lost her husband in the same week for goodness' sake. She deserved a spot of beauty in her life, and she wasn't the kind of person who'd appreciate the budget variety.

Connor thought she'd open up more without him being present so had taught us the kinds of questions that might elicit useful information. He would be waiting in his SUV nearby in case Handsome and Onion Head decided to drop by too.

The Watts' street in Pacific Palisades was just the way we'd left it after the emergency vehicles had disappeared.

Quiet, charming, serene. No hint at the recent violence and suffering going on behind the pretty, paneled windows of 1135. The gardener must have come this morning because not a single leaf broke the surface of the emerald-green lawn. Etta rang the doorbell.

We heard the clink of a keyhole cover shifting and slipping back into place before the door opened. Nicole looked ragged.

"We didn't exactly get to introduce ourselves yesterday," Etta said, "but we wanted to see how you were doing."

"Thank you. I keep thinking about what would've happened if you weren't there."

Her gratitude seemed genuine, but she didn't make any move to invite us in. Was she suspicious about how we'd happened to come to her rescue at the right moment? Please don't ask.

"How did you know something was wrong?" she asked.

Etta and I looked at each other.

"Oh," Etta said. "We overheard those men saying something about—well, it had a lot of swear words—as they left their car, and I'm a member of one of those neighborhood watch programs, so I thought we should check if everything was okay."

I was wondering how Etta was going to explain why our checking everything was okay involved creeping around the side of the house and peering in windows, but she didn't elaborate and Nicole seemed to accept the explanation.

"I'm glad you did."

She didn't shift from her position though. The door was a third of the way open, and she was squeezed into the gap. Almost like she was body-blocking us.

"We brought you these," I said, handing her the flowers. Maybe they'd get us inside.

"They're beautiful. Thank you." She held them awkwardly, apparently hoping we'd leave.

We didn't.

"I'm sorry, I'd invite you inside, but the house is in no state for visitors."

"I'll bet it can't be worse than Izzy's place." Etta sounded amused. "That's Isobel by the way, and I'm Etta. And I'm afraid this isn't just a social call. You see, those men, whoever they were, retaliated last night. They set fire to her apartment."

"Oh my gosh. I'm so sorry."

"It's not your fault. But anything you can tell us about them will help make sure they don't keep coming after us. Any of us."

Nicole's already slender figure seemed to shrink, and she finally stepped back. "You'd better come in."

The house was a complete disaster. No wonder she'd been blocking our view. Drawers had been emptied, furniture and couches overturned, and belongings piled in the middle of the floor. The thugs must have returned while she was in the hospital and torn the place up. Right before burning down my apartment.

They had been busy.

"Sorry about the mess," she said, limping ahead of us. She was wearing sandals that didn't touch her toes, and the digits that were missing nails were bandaged. "I've been trying to find what those men were looking for."

She'd done this herself?

"They sent me a message when I was at the hospital, saying if I don't find the stash or if I get the police involved again, they'd . . ." She took a moment to compose herself enough to continue. "They'd kill my son."

Uh-oh.

"Those dirty rotten scoundrels," Etta exclaimed. "Who the hell are they anyway?"

Nicole put the flowers on the counter and retrieved an expensive-looking vase from an overhead cupboard. "I don't know exactly. I'd never met them before yesterday, but they claimed to know Michael. That's my husband . . . I mean late husband. He was murdered a week ago." Her lip quivered as she filled the vase with water. "They were asking where his stash was, but I didn't know what they were talking about. They wouldn't believe me and kept saying how the boss didn't like loose ends."

"What kind of stash? Did they say?"

"Um." Tears shone in her eyes. "Sorry, it's hard for me to think about. The ugly one mentioned drugs at some point? But while my husband was many things, and not always the same person he liked to believe he was, to my knowledge he never touched drugs. He would even avoid taking medication prescribed by a doctor."

Etta bustled into the kitchen. "You poor dear. Go and sit down. I'll make us all a cup of tea."

Like a child, Nicole absently did as she was told.

"Did you find anything in your search?" I asked.

She screwed up her mouth. "Just a lot of dust. And I'm running out of places to look."

"Don't you worry about that. We'll figure this out," Etta said.

I wished she'd stop promising people that.

I wanted to help, but I was less optimistic about our ability to do it. Since I couldn't take her words back, I ran through the types of questions Connor had suggested might be enlightening.

Looking at the puzzle pieces, we were guessing that whatever those thugs were after, it was most likely related to Michael's covert activities. But Connor had explained that when someone is confronted with the possibility that their loved one is involved in some kind of scandal, their gut reaction is to deny it, and their mind scrambles to back that notion up. Which means if you ask them anything point- blank, you're not likely to get helpful answers.

However, if you approach it obliquely, you might uncover what the person knows without knowing they know. Connor had instructed me to ask about recent changes in behavior and to consider what the suspect would need. For example, supplies, contacts, times, locations, excuses, and that sort of thing, then ask general questions around that.

I took a deep breath and dived in. "Did your late husband—Michael—change his behavior lately? Like taking up a new routine or hobby? Or acting strangely?"

"Well, yes, I suppose so. He's never been very interested in our son Jaden. Michael's a tough disciplinarian, the same as his own father was. But this year he started taking Jaden to football practice. Michael had never done anything like that before, but I hoped it was because he'd realized he could relate more to Jaden now that he's growing up."

I thought about what football practice might have to do with drugs. Contacts? Supplies? "Did he get along with the other parents?" I asked. "Or anyone in particular?"

"I don't know. He didn't want me coming, so I stayed home. He told me he wanted some proper father-son time."

"How did Jaden react to it?"

"He wasn't so sure at first. As I said, Michael's always been tough on him. But after the first few times, he seemed okay with it."

"Did Mr. Watts bring anything with him to the games?" If he was dealing or picking up drugs, I figured he'd need something to carry them in.

"Yes. Jaden's gym bag and a cooler with a couple of beers."

"Have you looked in there for the stash?"

Her eyes widened, and she pushed herself up. "I'll do it now." She limped back a minute later with the two bags and plonked them on the table. We all peered in eagerly as she opened the gym bag, then reeled backward as she pulled out a pair of socks, stiff with sweat. "Sorry about that." Her cheeks went pink. "I didn't get around to doing the washing this week."

"No need to apologize," Etta told her.

Nicole disposed of the socks and kept digging. She pulled out a helmet, a red jersey, pants, shoulder pads, elbow pads, and pads for well, the family jewels, and a pair of cleats. No drugs. Emptied of its contents, the bag was so light that after a brief shake, we knew it couldn't be hiding anything in the lining. The cooler was empty too. I felt around the padded sides, feeling for anything amiss, but found nothing.

Damn.

Nicole sank back down in her chair, looking deflated.

But just because Michael hadn't kept the drugs in the bags didn't mean he hadn't put them in there at some point.

"Can you think of any other behavioral changes?" I asked.

She stared at the table. "He started going out more often after work. I thought maybe he was cheating on me, so I followed him a couple of times. On both occasions he went to a bar in Hollywood Heights and met with a man but someone different each time. I figured it must've been a business thing or his friends from work."

His mysterious meetings at the bar would've been an excellent setup to discreetly deal drugs. Small, dimly lit rooms with the view obscured by those brown leather couches. "Did he bring anything with him when he went to the bar?"

"No. I don't think so."

"Not a briefcase or something like that?"

She shook her head. "Nothing except his wallet."

I mulled that over. If my speculation about his purpose at the bar was correct, then he must have been dealing quantities small enough to fit in his pocket or wallet. But he had to keep the main supply somewhere. "Did he always take the same car?"

"Yes. I mean, we never swap cars, so yes."

That must be it. "Where is it?"

She put a hand to her throat. "The police have it. That's where he was . . . murdered." Then realization dawned. "You think whatever they're looking for is in his car?"

"Maybe. If he had a supply of drugs that he wasn't using, it follows that he must've been dealing them. His meetings at the bar would be a good place to hand them over to customers. But he would have needed to keep them somewhere, and the car's a logical choice. It would save him from sneaking them in and out past you and Jaden as well."

The pallor of her skin made her look ill. "If it's true, then I can't stop those men from going after Jaden. The police won't let me near it. I'm the spouse, which automatically makes me a suspect."

While it was nice to hear the LAPD had at least considered someone else as a possible suspect, it was going to make our search for the drugs impossible.

"We'll figure something out," Etta promised her again.

Suddenly my burned apartment no longer seemed like such a big problem.

———————

I WAS SCHEDULED TO SERVE Vanessa at yet another lunch date, but she texted me to say it had been canceled. The "friend" she'd been meeting had come down with food poisoning. Or more likely, an overdose of laxatives like the one Vanessa had narrowly avoided.

It was terrible to be glad of another's misfortune, but I took the news with relief. Connor had cleared his whole day to help solve the dangerous-thugs problem, and after the past twenty-four hours, the last thing I felt like was protecting Vanessa from paltry threats to her beauty.

Etta was less glad about it since she'd made plans with a friend for the hours I'd expected to be working. "Maybe I should cancel," she mused. "I'd hate to miss any of the action."

"You won't. This car-crime-scene issue is going to take ages for us to figure out a way around. If we figure it out at all. Besides, doing something completely different while your subconscious works away at it might give you the flash of inspiration we need."

She harrumphed but dropped me off where Connor was waiting and continued on to her date.

"How do we protect Nicole and Jaden?" I asked him when I climbed into the SUV.

"Long term, we need to find the drugs those men are so keen to get ahold of and give it back to them. Short term, I'll put a security detail on the Wattses."

"Wait, hand over the stash to the thugs? Why?"

"So we can find out who the hell their boss is and take all the bastards down together."

"Oh."

The trouble was, first we needed to find the aforementioned stash. Which was most likely in the car. Which was in police lockup.

"You're so lucky to have me," Connor said.

"Well sure, but which of your many virtues should I be thanking my lucky stars for now?"

"I might be able to get access to that car."

I wondered if he was pulling my leg, but that wasn't Connor's style. "Really? How?"

"Hunt."

He meant Police Commander Hunt. The one that probably used my face for target practice.

"He hates you almost as much as he hates me. What makes you think he'll give you access to a crime scene that's got nothing to do with the Taste Society?"

"Because I have good reason to believe that it does have something to do with the Taste Society. From what we know, there are illicit drugs and poisons in that crime scene. Watts would have had to shift large quantities of recreational drugs to make enough money to make it worth his while, and his lack of repeat customers don't fit the pattern of addictive street drugs. Given his clientele and his behavior, I'd say there's a good chance he was selling customized poisons to his rich and powerful friends."

I hadn't given much thought to how the rich and

famous acquired their weapon of choice. It made sense that there had to be dealers.

"Will it be enough to convince Hunt to help?" I asked.

"It's part of our cooperation agreement that the liaison will assist us in taking that type of thing out of circulation. It's not like I'm trying to take over his case."

I bit my lip. "Um. There might be a problem."

"What?"

"Etta and I kind of went to the police station hoping to get some information from a sympathetic officer. Instead, I spoke to Hunt, who of course got it into his head that I was interfering with his case."

"You are."

"That's beside the point. The point is, he might be suspicious of your motives now, and if he ever realizes we're dating, you could be compromising that important liaison relationship."

Connor's lips thinned. "Then we better find those damn poisons."

17

CONNOR HAD BEEN USING the term "we" loosely. I would make myself scarce while he approached Hunt about searching the car. Since I couldn't imagine the police had cleaned the blood and brain matter off the seat, I was secretly grateful I had a reason to stay away. Connor dropped me at my apartment to continue taking stock of everything that would need to be done.

Mostly, I just sat down on an unburned patch of the floor and felt overwhelmed. Then I worked up the courage to call the landlord and break the news to my housemate, Oliver.

Because the events—despite what Connor was telling Hunt—had nothing to do with the secretive Taste Society, and because Etta knew the true version already, for once I didn't have to lie to Oliver. When I'd finished recounting the whole story and reassuring him that Meow and all the belongings in his room were okay, I sucked in some breaths and waited. I'm not sure what I was expecting. Cursing? A rant about the Queen not having to deal with this kind of thing? But I could never have anticipated his actual reaction.

He laughed. An uncontrollable, high-pitched, eyes-streaming sort of laugh that had me wondering if he was hysterical. "You"—he managed to get out—"let Etta"—more laughter—"talk you into that?"

I waited for his chortling to subside. "I don't see what's so funny. Did you miss the bit where our apartment almost burned down?"

"S-sorry." He choked down more laughter. "I'm sure it must've been a very traumatic experience. But I can't believe you and Etta fancy yourselves detectives!"

It sounded like he was in danger of bursting from his mirth.

"I do not! Etta guilted me into attempting to help. I told her it was a bad idea, but I never thought it would turn out this bad. You get that everything in the living area will need replacing, right?"

"Sure," he said, still giggling. "Tough luck, but most of that furniture was junk anyway."

"I take it you didn't bother to get renters insurance then?"

He laughed some more, which I took to mean no.

I let out a beleaguered sigh. "All right. Well. I'm glad you're not upset. And I'll make sure it's fixed by the time you get back."

"Brilliant. See you soon, Iz."

I hung up the phone, not feeling nearly as relieved as it seemed I should. Despite Oliver's amusement, I suspected he'd feel differently when he got home to an unfamiliar apartment. He was sentimental and oddly attached to inanimate objects for the memories they held.

He'd kept the first toy he'd ever bought for Meow, even after it broke and Meow would no longer acknowledge its existence. He had a lucky T-shirt that was so worn it was see-through, which he still brought out on special occasions. And while most of the furniture had been old, shabby, and left behind by previous tenants moving onto better things, Oliver had fond memories of some of those housemates. Unimpressed by brands or wealth or style, he put much more value on shared experience than what society said something was worth. He'd gone so far as to keep the letters from the ex-girlfriend who'd broken his heart because he hadn't wanted to throw the good times out with the bad. The more I thought about it, the more guilty I felt about ruining his sanctum of memories.

Connor rescued me from my musings with a text.

Found drugs under a false bottom in the center console. See you in ten.

Not for the first time, I wondered how he knew where I was before remembering the GPS tracking app he had on my phone. It was a little unnerving to think he could always find me, but it had saved my life at least once. Hard to argue with that.

I was piling all the items that would need to be thrown out in the middle of the living area so I could figure out what size dumpster to hire, when Connor found me. He was immaculate. I was covered in black filth.

He slipped three capsules out of his pocket. "Can you identify what these are?"

I stared at him. "They've got pocket lint on them."

He looked me over in all my sooty glory, a smile tugging at the edges of his mouth, then made a show of brushing them off. "Now can you identify them? The LAPD wouldn't let me take any so I had to sneak them out. They'll take at least a month to finish testing them, and I wanted to know what we were dealing with before then. Like, today."

"Let me wash up first."

I chose one of the capsules at random, pulled it apart, and sampled the powder inside. It was a custom cocktail of opioids. I couldn't really tell which ones, and I didn't need to. Some classes of drugs share a distinct taste and the same antidote, so we didn't waste energy distinguishing them. Despite their bitter taste, opioids were a favorite of poisoners since every year in the US alone fourteen thousand people died of an overdose on the prescription kind, and a similar number died from the illicit kind. In most cases, the police wouldn't dig too deep.

A lump formed in my throat. It was opioids that had killed my last client. Whoever was concocting this stuff needed to be taken down.

The second pill was a highly concentrated blood pressure drug. It wasn't likely to kill the average person, but it would be lethal to someone already on heart medication. And if it was the same type the intended victim was prescribed, cause of death would probably be deemed an accidental overdose. That was if they bothered to test for the drug in the first place.

I tasted the contents of the last capsule. Lithax. It was another popular choice for professional poisoners but a nonlethal one. It was formulated from three prescription drugs to cause a rapid decrease in lithium levels, which would cause the target to have a manic or depressive attack. In rare cases it could lead to suicide, but most of the time it was used to stop the person from being able to function at a high-stakes event. Technically, there were lots of drug combinations that could do the same thing, but this was the only known blend that tasted mild enough to disguise in food. Hence its popularity.

It was a sober reminder of what a Shade is usually up against. For all the pressure brought on by Vanessa's expectations and strong personality, the stakes were low. I should be grateful for the mini-holiday.

Connor was leaning on a clean patch of wall wearing his no-nonsense business face. The blood pressure pill must have felt too close to home after his mom's recent heart scare. The way the opioids had been for me.

"Thank you," he said. "That confirms our suspicions that Watts was dealing high-end custom poisons. And that he wouldn't have been able to make them himself, which means the person who did is likely to be the same person who hired criminals to retrieve them. I suspect we're looking for a professional in the medical industry given that they'd need a background in chemistry and access to prescription drugs."

"Agreed. But that doesn't narrow it down enough for us to identify them."

"That's where our pyromaniac thugs come in." He pulled out a small black money belt. "The police let me take this, which is what we found the poisons in. And I have photos of its contents, which I sent to the research team so they can find substitutes that'll pass a quick inspection."

"Hunt really let you take it?"

"Don't sound so surprised. He's a decent detective, but he doesn't know what you and I got up to in bed this morning."

My cheeks heated, and Connor's business face softened. But the poison was too fresh on my tongue to get sidetracked.

"So we get Nicole to give Handsome and Onion Head the money belt with its fake drugs," I guessed, "and they lead us to whoever hired them."

Connor nodded. "And with nicknames like that, I can't wait to meet these guys."

———

CONNOR AND I HAD LUNCH at a sushi bar while the research team did their part. Over the salmon sashimi, I coaxed him into talking to me. Any personal topic of his choice, as long as it wasn't about work. He tried. He really did. But within three sentences, he'd lapsed back into discussing the case.

Well, it was a start. And it was more than I'd ever managed to get from my Taste Society handler Jim.

The thugs had thoughtfully provided a contact number by texting threatening messages to Nicole. So when we were ready, she replied to the last threat to say she'd located what they were looking for and placed it in the letterbox.

Connor, Etta, and I were in separate vehicles so we could take turns tailing them without being obvious about it. Because they knew my car and Etta's yellow Dodge Charger was too noticeable, we were borrowing cars from Connor's security company.

At the moment, we were all doing laps of the block after deciding a parked car would be too suspicious if Handsome and Onion Head were feeling wary. I hoped they'd arrive promptly, or we were going to waste a lot of fuel and make the residents suspicious instead. Given the extreme measures the men had taken, Connor was confident they'd respond fast.

A familiar black sedan rolled down the street. Each of Connor's vehicles had Bluetooth audio and microphones, so we were sharing a three-way call. "They're here," I reported, cruising past them as they stopped at the letterbox. "Heading east as long as they don't do a U-turn."

"Good. Izzy, get out of sight. Etta, you take the first stretch."

"Right on," Etta said, excitement coloring her voice. "I can see them now. Onion Head is returning from the letterbox and re-entering the car."

That was excellent news. We'd thought that once they got what they wanted, they might pay Nicole another visit to make sure she never talked.

"They're heading east like Izzy said. Taking a right-hand turn at the T-junction. Since there's not much other traffic around here, I think one of you should take over as soon as we hit a main road."

"Good," Connor said. "You turn the opposite direction whenever that happens, and I'll take over for the next stretch."

We continued on in this fashion, the two nonactive tails staying farther behind, until our unsuspecting goons pulled up outside an inconspicuous house in Mid-City. After meeting Madam Devine and now this, I'd never look at a quiet, inconspicuous suburban house the same way again.

I was tailing them when they stopped, so I drove past and parked on the next street. Etta joined me a minute later.

"Now what?"

We all knew she was asking Connor rather than me. "Sit tight. I'm going in." He disconnected.

Etta and I looked at each other from our separate vehicles. "I don't like this," she said.

I squelched down my own misgivings. "He's a professional. He does this kind of thing all the time."

"Yeah, well professionals die all the time."

"Etta!"

"What? It's like you said, even professional detectives have partners. He needs backup, and I'm going to give it to him." She slid out the car, toting her Glock.

Groaning, I slid out after her and grabbed my Taser for

good measure. Connor would be pissed, but I was concerned about what she'd get up to without my supervision. I texted him a warning as we walked.

Etta doesn't understand how to "sit tight." We're coming on foot.

He replied seconds later.

Dammit. They know what you look like. Stay out of sight.

I pointed this out to Etta. "Huh. Guess I should've brought my harmless-old-lady disguise. We'll have to go approach from the neighboring yard."

Her words reminded me of my and Connor's conversation this morning, and I couldn't resist texting him back.

If only I'd grown that genius mustache so they wouldn't recognize me.

He didn't send me a smiley face. Connor didn't smile even in emoji form.

They're taking the money belt inside and handing it over to another man. I've requested police backup.

I relayed this to Etta, but she didn't slow down. "Police backup might not come fast enough."

I had no choice but to keep following her. My phone buzzed again.

Damn. The new guy knocked out the two thugs with some type of gas bomb. I'll have to go in and rescue their sorry asses.

Wait. I texted him. We might be able to help.

Half a minute later, we reached the neighboring property and could just see into the target's windows if we peered over the fence. I couldn't spot Handsome and Onion Head from this vantage point, but I assumed they were on the floor. A petite, bespectacled man was moving around, a gas mask hanging loose at his neck, and what appeared to be rope in his hands.

Connor burst into the room like some kind of action hero, and I wanted to wring his neck for not waiting and take him to bed for being so freaking attractive.

The petite man dropped the rope. But instead of surrendering, he slipped his gas mask on. With a sinking sensation, I realized he must've thrown down another gas concoction along with that rope.

Connor seemed unaffected so far. He was smart enough to hold his breath. But for how long?

The other guy wasn't equipped to deal with a conscious opponent. He backed away, hands raised. Connor stalked forward to take him down, and I felt some of the tension ease out of me as the man behind the mask stayed submissive, arms safely over his head.

Until Connor doubled over from a knee to his groin.

To my horror, I watched the wrong man fall.

Panic flashed through me as Connor disappeared from view. The pain would've made him gasp, which would've made him inhale the gas. What if it did worse than knock someone out?

What if—

"Hell," Etta said like she was contemplating a rat that needed killing. "This is why you need a backup partner."

Her words seeped through my hysteria. The petite man picked up the rope again. Ropes were for tying. He wouldn't need to tie someone up if they were dead. Right?

Unless—

No. I couldn't afford to think that way. I wouldn't.

"Okay," I said, sucking in deep breaths and trying to force my brain out of its panicked loop onto a more useful train of thought. We had to take this bastard down so I could get to Connor. But how? I wouldn't do Connor any good if I ended up passed out on the floor beside him. "We're going to have to take this guy by surprise in case he has any more of those knockout bombs up his sleeve."

Etta raised her Glock. "Or we could shoot him."

"No!" I pushed her arm back down. Carefully. "Well . . . not except as a last resort."

She sighed and slipped the weapon into her bag. "Your generation always wants to complicate things. Did you bring your Taser?"

"Yes." I'd known this wasn't going to go well.

"Good. Then I'll go break a window in another part of the house. While Scrawny Scientist over there goes to investigate, you open one of the other windows and taser him when he comes back."

"What if I can't open one of them from the outside?"

"Break it."

"But then he'll know I'm there."

"Sneak in through the front door and hide behind the couch then."

"He'll hear me. I don't know which floorboards creak or hinges squeak or—"

"If he comes after you, I'll shoot him."

And we were back to the shooting. I tried to think. "Wait, what if we just ring the doorbell and taser him when he comes to answer it?"

"What if he doesn't come to the door?"

"We'll think up a plan B."

"What if you miss? Or if he throws one of those chemical doodads down before you get the chance?"

I eyed her. "You can stand off to the side, out of range of the chemical doodads, and shoot him."

She fingered her Glock and smiled. "That might just work."

———

AS THE PETITE MAN WRITHED on the floor in front of me, I realized we should've discussed what to do if the plan worked.

The Taser charge would last thirty seconds. Time that Connor had always told me to use to run away. But I couldn't run away on this occasion, and we had to secure the guy's hands before he regained control over his muscles and let off another one of those knockout bombs.

I sprinted for the rope I'd seen him with, holding my breath as I entered the room and grabbed it off the floor. My instincts screamed at me to go to Connor's still form, but I resisted and sprinted back again.

"Wait!" Etta shouted as I bent down to tie him. "Won't you get shocked too?"

Crap. I didn't know. "I have to risk it."

If I failed, Etta could shoot him before he got a chance to attack. I braced myself and touched his arm. Nothing. The Taser charge finished a few seconds later. I grabbed his hands and yanked the rope around them. It was hard with my own shaking. Thank goodness Scrawny Scientist wasn't recovering well. His limbs were weak and unresisting, the gas mask hanging ineffectually from his neck.

In the movies they always make it look easy to tie up a man. But I hadn't tied up anything except my shoelaces in years, and it was harder than it looked. Etta was still standing at a distance, out of chemical range. I used my knee to hold down one end of the rope while I wound the other tightly around his wrists. I wasn't sure how easy it would be for him to set off another nasty surprise, so I levered him over to get the rope around his back, strapping his wrists to his own body, before tying the knot away from his hands so he couldn't undo it. I didn't know any fancy knots, so I did the most basic one over and over again. Guess I should've been a Girl Scout after all.

Hoping it wouldn't just unravel of its own accord, I yelled at Etta to watch him and sprinted back to Connor. He was propped up on one elbow, trying to sit up. Relief washed over me.

"Are you okay?" I asked.

I'll admit it. I experienced a flash of satisfaction from asking him that question instead of the other way around for a change.

He grunted. "Where's—?"

"Tied up by the front door."

Onion Head moaned. After two doses of whatever our gas-wielding wacko had used, they were slower to wake up. But they'd be a problem when they did.

"I think we better tie these guys too," I said reluctantly. If Connor wasn't well enough to do the deed, it was going to be downright embarrassing with him watching on.

He pushed himself all the way upright. "I'll deal with them. You better go ask that other one any questions you have before the police arrive. Based on this"—he gestured at the three of them felled on the floor—"I'm guessing he's the chemist behind the operation. The one your victim was dealing with."

Seeing that Connor was going to be okay, I took the reprieve gladly. Besides, Hunt wouldn't let me near Scrawny Scientist once they had him in custody.

The ropes had remained intact, and he was looking more alert when I returned to the doorstep. Sirens sounded in the distance.

"Did you kill Michael Watts? Or arrange for him to be killed?" I asked.

"I'm gonna kill you, bitch," he sneered.

At least now I didn't feel bad about tasering him.

I positioned a knee over his groin. "Look, that's my boyfriend you kneed in the crotch in there. I'm happy to return the favor if you don't start talking."

He tried to spit at me. Maybe if he hadn't been tasered mere minutes ago it would have hit me in the face, but the soggy globule only made it half the height before landing harmlessly on his shirt.

Etta abandoned her chemical-safe distance and shoved her Glock in his face. "What were you saying?"

His face went red with rage, but he muttered the answer through clenched teeth. "I didn't kill Michael. He was my friend."

"Then why'd you let your thugs torture your friend's wife?" I asked.

"I didn't specify to torture her. That's on them. I just told them to get the damn stash back so no one could follow it to me."

I didn't tell him they'd burned my apartment too. He'd probably be glad to hear it. Besides, the sirens' wailing was growing louder and time was short. "Why did Watts agree to peddle poisons for you? What was in it for him?"

He looked at me like I was the dumbest thing he'd ever laid eyes on. "Money. Same as me."

"He's rich. Why would he need the money?"

He wriggled himself upright until Etta's gun pressed to his forehead. "Why would he need the money? Are you kidding? You stupid women don't know what it's like for us. We're expected to provide everything you ever desire, and you have no idea how stressful that is. Michael's business wasn't going well, and he needed to alleviate some of that stress. He was fond of doing that with girls who do as they're told and don't judge you for it." He sneered at me. "Not like you self-entitled bitches. So he needed money that couldn't be traced, and since everyone pays for poison in untraceable cash, it was perfect."

"Until he was killed," I pointed out.

Vehicles screeched to a stop, and car doors thudded, but I had what I needed from him. As loathsome as he was, he wasn't Michael's shooter.

"What were you going to do with your hired thugs?" I asked out of curiosity as a group of police ordered Etta to put her weapon down and all of us to raise our hands in the air. Scrawny Scientist was going to have trouble following that order.

"I don't like loose ends," he hissed at me, eyes full of hate.

The police officers streamed toward us. "Well," I said. "The only loose end you need to deal with now is how you're gonna stop your hired thugs from killing you in prison."

Once we'd given our statements about a dozen times, the officers informed us we were free to go. Connor had been assessed by first responders and was looking pale but otherwise okay.

"So now that you've proven you can protect me physically," he said, "does that mean I don't have to share things of an emotional nature with you anymore?"

I glared at him. "Careful. If I can protect you, I might be able to hurt you too." In contradiction to my threat, I couldn't resist stepping forward and hugging him tightly. I'd been so scared for him.

He returned my embrace. "I'm glad you're safe." It was as if he stole the sentiment right out of my head. "But now that you are, I have work I need to catch up on. See you later tonight, okay?"

I would've loved to unwind with him, to spend time in his presence doing mundane things to reassure myself he was really unscathed. But he'd already given me an entire day out of his busy schedule and lost another recently to keep his mom company in the hospital. Reassuring myself would have to wait.

We kissed goodbye, sending heat sizzling all the way down to my toes. Then Etta and I trudged back to our cars and drove to Connor's place in Beverly Hills. Etta to do a car swap, and me because it was my and Meow's temporary home.

Etta's eyes were burning with curiosity at the Tudor mansion. This afternoon was the first occasion she'd ever been on the property, and we hadn't had time to do anything but switch cars and head straight to Nicole's.

"Would you like to come in?" I asked after an internal tug of war. I wasn't comfortable treating the house as my own, but it felt wrong to send her on her way without a drink to celebrate today's victory.

A victory that sadly brought us no closer to clearing Mr. Black's name.

Etta grabbed my arm and tugged me toward the front door. "You already know the answer to that."

Mae was in the kitchen cooking dinner, Meow rubbing against her ankles. I was busting for the toilet, so I made introductions and then left them to get to know each other while I relieved myself. When I returned, Etta was telling Mae a highly embellished version of today's events. Though when she got to the part with Scrawny Scientist, she didn't need to embellish it much.

Mae took the recounting of her son's lifeless body on the floor very well. Maybe because she already knew the happy ending. Or maybe because in her own life as a private investigator and having a military man as a husband she'd found some way of dealing with her loved ones being in danger.

That and Etta's enthusiasm in the vivid retelling was contagious.

She was up to the bit where she'd been struggling to hold her gun steady while laughing at my inept efforts to tie a rope when her phone rang. The conversation was short, and when she disconnected, her expression was sober. "That was Abe. The police just found the murder weapon in his home."

18

ETTA FLOORED IT to the Blacks' home, and we found them huddled around the small round dining table, looking shell-shocked.

"It's not mine," Mr. Black said.

Hallie and Joy answered in perfect sync. "We know."

I had the distinct impression this same exchange had been stuck on repeat for a while.

The police had searched the Blacks' residence after an anonymous tip and found what was most likely the murder weapon. It was unregistered, wiped clean, and the same caliber as the gun that had shot Michael Watts in the head. It was also the one piece of evidence the LAPD needed to wrap up their case as far as they were concerned. The sole reason Mr. Black wasn't back in jail was they needed ballistics to confirm it first.

"I don't even carry a gun," Mr. Black said. "You know that, Ms. Avery."

Somehow I'd overlooked that when I'd been running for my life and when I'd first heard the details of the case. But now that he mentioned it, I couldn't remember seeing him with a gun. If he'd had a gun, he wouldn't have been swayed by my Taser. If he'd had a gun, he wouldn't have had to bother chasing me down the street. And even if he did have a gun, I couldn't believe he'd be so stupid as to murder someone with it and then bring it to his family home. It was too convenient. All of a sudden, our assumption that Mr. Black had just been in the wrong place at the wrong time seemed incorrect.

Yes. The more I thought about it, the more I was convinced Mr. Black had been set up to take the fall. And I was damned if I was going to let them get away with it.

The one positive side was it might help us narrow down our list of suspects.

"Where exactly did they find the gun?" I asked.

"Hidden in the bookshelf."

"How possible would it be for someone to have snuck in and planted it without you noticing?"

Hallie answered. "Almost impossible, I'd think. I've been here all day, every day, and I know every groan and creak this house makes. I think I'd hear if there was an intruder. Unless we were asleep, but then the doors would've been locked."

"We need a list of people who've visited you in the week since the murder."

"We've had a few neighbors and friends drop off food, but aside from yourselves, there have only been three who came inside. Principal Gibson came after she heard Abe had been arrested to talk about how the other kids would react when the news got out and how to minimize the negative effect it would have on Joy. Mr. Bergström came over to fire Abe three days ago. And my best friend has come over a few times, but there's no way it was her."

We shared a pot of tea and caught them up on what we'd learned so far. Most of it had been a dead end, but the gun being planted gave us new leads.

"It has to be Bergström," I told Etta on the way home. "He's one of the few people who had the chance to plant the murder weapon. Plus he was the one who sent Mr. Black after Michael Watts in the first place, then denied it to the police. The only thing I'm not clear on is motive."

"We also have the problem that we don't have a scrap of evidence to support it."

She was right. In fact, all the evidence pointed to Mr. Black. His DNA on the victim, a witness seeing him leaving the scene within the time-of-death window, and now the murder weapon found in his home. It would be an open-and-shut case in front of a jury unless we could prove someone else did it.

"So how do we track down some evidence and a motive?" I asked, my deductions about Bergström seeming a whole lot less groundbreaking now.

"By tracking the slimy bastard himself," Etta muttered.

Remembering his gun and the armchair-man bodyguard, I had a bad feeling about that.

Unfortunately, I didn't have any better suggestions.

———

CONNOR WAS STILL OUT WORKING when I got home and gone again before I got up. It was New Year's Eve, and the only proof of him having slept beside me was a sleep-muddled memory of being held in his arms. His side of the bed was neatly made, of course.

Would I get to see him tonight? I felt bad that protecting me had put him so far behind that he couldn't take New Year's Eve off to spend with his mom. And me. Not that I didn't have my own share of work for the day.

Mae and I shared chocolate croissants for breakfast.

"Are you as neat as Connor is?" I asked her after I'd caught her up on the Black case.

"No. He gets that from his father. He was an army man and liked his belongings organized just so. It's about survival out there when a second of looking for something you misplaced could cost you everything, but it becomes a way of life."

I nodded, immediately feeling bad for all the times I'd teased Connor about it—even if most of those times had been in my head.

"Don't look so grim. I never stop missing Emmett, but I've had more than two decades to learn how to live with it. I like talking about him, you know? Remembering all those great years we shared."

I let her words sink in. "In that case, Connor once mentioned that you met when you were paid to investigate him on a PI case. I'd love to hear the story if you feel like sharing."

She beamed. "That's one of my favorites. It was over forty years ago. We were both so young, in our early twenties. My grandfather was a cop, who got injured and became a PI rather than being relegated to desk duty. That's how I got into it. So when this animal rights activist came in and asked him to gather evidence to help take down an exotic bird smuggler, Gramps took on the case. He tailed the main suspect and assigned me to follow Emmett. The client thought he might've been involved because he knew the head smuggler and had done a tour of duty in one of the countries the birds were being smuggled from, but Gramps figured it was a long shot.

"The first look I got at Emmett I was blown away. He was so handsome. I thought I'd landed the cushiest job in the world—staring at that face and body all day." She laughed at herself. "Only Emmett caught on that he was being watched. Maybe I'd been getting closer than I should because I wanted a better view. Or maybe he was just smarter than your average surveillance subject. One day, I lost sight of him for a minute and was panicking, thinking I might've lost him right before the big exchange, when he knocked on my window. I must've jumped so high I hit my head on the roof. It was a cute little Fiat. Anyway, I rolled my window down since what else could I do? And he said, 'How did I manage to get a pretty girl like you following me around?' I almost died of embarrassment, but at the same time, a voice in my head was whooping about how he thought I was pretty. Out loud, I burbled something about not knowing what he was talking about and drove straight back to Gramps and told him I'd been sprung.

"It was days later after the case was wrapped up— Emmett wasn't involved by the way—that I ran into him outside the movie theater. And he smiled and said, 'I've missed seeing you.' He asked me to watch The Shining with him, and that was that." Her eyes shone with tears. "He loved telling that tale. He'd tell it to complete strangers if he got half the chance. He'd recount it with such pride too. I never knew if it was pride for his spunky wife who had such an unusual job or pride in himself for spotting me. Maybe it was both."

I hugged her. "That's an amazing story. I can see why it's one of your favorites. Thank you for sharing it with me."

"Thanks for listening. As I said, it's nice to remember those things."

I wondered how I'd ended up with so many incredible female role models. My mother, Etta, and now Connor's mother as well.

No wonder I had self-esteem issues.

———

TO ENACT OUR MASTER PLAN of surveilling Bergström and proving Mr. Black's innocence, we needed three things: disguises, a small fleet of different cars, and a whole lotta junk food. Etta set about purchasing the junk food part of the equation along with large sunglasses and wigs to conceal our features, while I met with Harper to see if I could secure vehicles. I would've asked Connor, except his company cars only came in one variety: black. I suspected Mr. Bergström was smarter than your average thug. Plus I had yet to see Connor since we'd taken down Scrawny Scientist yesterday—unless you counted when I was asleep.

Harper grinned at me after I finished explaining the whole story. "Sure. I can help with that. Just don't crash them or get shot at or anything. And maybe don't tell Connor I helped you either."

I extended my hand. "You've got a deal."

Connor's family was turning out to be very useful for this case I'd never intended to take on. While Harper was loaning us the means of subtle surveillance, Mae had given us a high-zoom camera and was running background checks on Bergström and the victim to see if she could find any links between them. She was delighted to be involved in a way that even her overprotective son couldn't consider dangerous.

Etta and I reconvened at our apartment building in Palms and loaded our supplies into the car Harper had loaned us. Etta had purchased a blond wig for herself and a black wig for me. With my pale skin, it made me look like I was a member of the Goth subculture. But at least I didn't look like myself. Dudley was harder to disguise, but he was happy to lie down out of sight most of the time. Especially for a share of the junk food.

All revved up, we found Bergström leaving his office in Redondo Junction and followed him. He went to a coffee place, purchased a newspaper, and sat there for two hours. Then he went back to his office and sat there for three hours.

If the last two days had taught me anything, it was not to complain about boring surveillance. Boring was good. Boring was safe. Even so, boring was boring.

And if nothing happened, we were no closer to finding out why Bergström was framing Mr. Black or uncovering any proof beyond our own suspicions. Was it somehow related to the poisons Watts had been involved with? Was it personal? A debt that needed to be paid in blood? It didn't make any sense. There were no connections between Mr. Black's boss and the murder victim. They moved in utterly different circles. Where would they even chance upon each other?

Etta kept glancing at her bag, and I guessed it was for the pack of cigarettes inside. "I need the nicotine hit to keep me awake," she said when she saw me watching her. "You'd think following a crook around would be more fun."

Wordlessly, I passed her the pack of nicotine gum she'd left in the center console.

She snatched it from me with more force than necessary, popped one into her mouth, and proceeded to chew it viciously. "I can't believe I canceled my New Year's Eve plans for this."

"Look, he's moving," I said, mostly to take her mind off it. Bergström was moving, but only toward the bathroom.

Never mind that I hadn't had any New Year's Eve plans to cancel.

Etta made a noise of disgust. "And you tried to talk me out of this surveillance stuff because it might be dangerous. This is even more boring than daytime television!"

"We did face down two thugs who were torturing someone forty-eight hours ago," I reminded her.

She folded her arms across her chest. "Yes, but that was forty-eight hours ago."

19

WITH JUST ONE DAY BEFORE the Scandalous
Cause photo shoot, Vanessa had instructed me to be on
the very top of my game. A challenge with everything else
going on. So it was with some suspicion that I watched
Emily approach me as I headed to the kitchen for more
food.

"Do you ever stop to think that our clients are crazy?"
she asked in a quiet undertone.

I snuck a glance. Her expression was friendly instead of
snarky. Could we have finally found our common ground?
Was she using the new year to make a fresh start?

"All the time," I admitted.

"I don't know that Miranda has a single person she can
trust. Not even her husband or her own children."

I hesitated but couldn't see the harm in agreeing with her. "Vanessa's the same. You'd think it would bring them together. In their position I'd love to have a group of women to talk to and find comfort in."

"Ah, but that would require them to be vulnerable." She pursed her lips as if she'd been sucking on a lemon and affected a posh tone. "They're far too busy boasting about how wonderful their lives are."

I shook my head. "What's the point? Surely it's obvious that none of them are happy. Miranda is lonely, Stephanie feels like she's not good enough, Chloe is bored with her life, and Vanessa hates that open-marriage arrangement."

We'd reached the kitchen. The one Emily had gotten me banned from. "Look," she said, seeming embarrassed. "I'm sorry about . . . everything. I couldn't believe it when you helped me out after all of that. What did you want next? I'll grab it for you."

I'd picked out each course earlier when I'd scoured the menu. Vanessa had warned me to stay away from anything fattening today, so I said, "The roasted squash and charred radicchio salad."

She smiled like she was relieved and came back a minute later with the dish. "I won't be offended if you taste it."

"Thanks," I said, balancing the plate on the rim of the floor vase I'd been using as a makeshift table to do exactly that. No matter how nice she was being, I wasn't about to take any risks. I even tasted an extra couple of sections at random just to be certain. It was clear.

Maybe Emily really had changed her mind about me. We walked upstairs together, placed the salads in front of our clients, and resumed our positions.

Emily gave me the faintest of nods.

———

AS ETTA AND I RETURNED to surveilling Bergström, I reminded myself that there were some significant advantages over this versus working at the WECS Club. I could sit down. I didn't have to wear heels. And I needn't worry about poisons. But without the slightest suggestion of a lead so far, my apartment in ruins, and a sleep deficit to catch up on, it was hard to convince myself it was the best use of time.

Especially when the stupid wig Etta had picked out for me was so itchy. Even Dudley had decided to stay home and nap this round.

And we were doing it all for Mr. Black; the man I only knew because he'd been hired to beat me to a pulp.

The problem was, it wasn't all for him. It was for Hallie and Joy too, and no matter how I felt about Mr. Black, he shouldn't go to prison for a crime he didn't commit. Plus the more I saw him around his family and Etta, the less

I could see him as some kind of inhuman monster who deserved what he got.

He loved his family deeply. He'd never wanted to get into the debt collector business. Hell, a couple of weeks ago I'd even learned he was scared of blood. It was getting hard to hang on to my grudge faced with all of that.

Which made this surveillance more important and the lack of anything happening more worrisome.

Bergström was sitting in a Lebanese restaurant, taking his sweet time over the menu. Since I was stuck eating junk food or the crappy remains of trail mix Etta and I had already picked over, it was infuriating to watch. Not that I didn't love junk food, but I'd passed my limit hours earlier.

I scratched my scalp carefully, trying not to dishevel the wig. Could he turn those pages any slower?

A quarter of an hour later, Etta and I stared in shock as the lovely Principal Olivia Gibson made her way unhesitatingly over to Mr. Black's former boss. Like she knew where he was sitting. Like they did this regularly. Bergström got to his feet and they embraced. Not a sexy embrace but certainly not a business one either. I glanced over at Etta. "Are you seeing what I'm seeing?"

"Don't be fooled by my recent old-lady acting, dear. My eyes work just fine."

I rolled my own eyes before focusing back on the couple, who had sat down and were talking to the waitress.

"This is our missing link. It's got to be."

"If you ever lose your job as a honeytrap, you could go into the business of stating the obvious since it seems you're so great at it."

Okay, apparently hours of surveillance were not good for our relationship.

"But what does it mean? Why would Principal Gibson possibly want Watts dead? Do you think he did something to her? Threaten her maybe? Or disagree with her plans for some new school development?"

"Could have," Etta agreed. "Or they might've been lovers and it went wrong. Or perhaps one of the custom drugs he sold hurt someone close to her and she found out about it. But then where does Bergström come into it, and why frame Abe?"

"We should ask the Blacks. Maybe they'll have a few ideas."

Etta spat her gum into a tissue and looked at me. "And you should ask Mae to run a background check on Bergström and Gibson. If we find out how they know each other, the answer might become more clear."

I hoped a background check would turn up something helpful this time. The single link Mae had found between Bergström and Michael Watts was their star sign; they were both Taurus.

I hadn't bothered to consult their horoscope.

WE WATCHED Gibson and Bergström as they shared dinner, but we couldn't overhear their conversation and they didn't appear to exchange any packages. In other words, we didn't learn anything.

It looked like a friendly meal between two friends. Yet it was too coincidental to be meaningless. Etta was busting to get a table so we could eavesdrop, but I vetoed the idea because our disguises wouldn't have held up to that level of scrutiny. She had to content herself with making use of Mae's high-zoom camera.

After she'd taken about twenty boring shots of the pair of them, she moved on to photographing bald spots, crotch scratchers, and nose pickers.

I called Mae as Etta snickered beside me and asked her to look into Gibson and Bergström's backgrounds.

When our surveillance subjects eventually finished their meal, we tailed after Gibson. Perhaps for no other reason than we'd been following Bergström all day and were sick of the sight of his pale head.

Gibson drove to Los Feliz and pulled into the driveway of a neat single-story. The homes here were pleasantly middle class, sandwiched together with little room in between. The place our suspect was entering had a fenced yard, a rarity on this street where many of the houses were built inches from the sidewalk and tall shrubs to offer privacy from neighbors and passersby. Judging by the executive-looking satchel she carried inside, and the keys she procured from her bag, we figured it was where she called home.

"Should we wait and see if anything else happens tonight?" I asked, stretching my legs in the hope of preventing further butt cramps.

Etta shook her head. "She's putting all the blinds down anyway. Let's go and find out what the Blacks know about the principal of their fancy school."

The Black residence looked even more shabby in comparison to Gibson's well-maintained one. But it was filled with love and warmth, rather than potential murderers.

Only Hallie was home. Joy was at a friend's for a sleepover. A friend from elementary school, not the Frederick Academy.

We'd just sat down around the dining table when Mr. Black came through the front door. I was glad to see him because it meant he wasn't in prison yet. Perhaps it being New Year's Eve had slowed down getting results on that ballistics test.

He took one look at us and moved to the freshly boiled kettle. "I'll make tea."

"Have you ever seen or heard of Principal Gibson involved in anything suspicious?" I asked them.

"Olivia?" Hallie said, incredulous. "No, she's always been lovely to us. And I'm not saying that lightly. Some of the teachers at the Frederick Academy seem to think Joy doesn't deserve to be there because we don't have as much money as the other children's parents, can you believe? I mean, in what distorted world does that make sense?"

The same world where it made sense to poison one another for the dubious honor of posing nude in the Scandalous Cause calendar, I supposed.

"But Olivia is super supportive and has forced them to treat Joy fairly. She's even held information nights showing documentaries on kids who grew up in rough circumstances but got a scholarship and ended up having a huge positive impact on society. Of course, none of the parents who are against the idea bothered to attend, but she made it mandatory for the teachers."

Dammit, I was starting to like the woman.

"And then, as I told you, when she heard Abe had been arrested, she visited us to talk with Joy about how to deal with the repercussions of the news at school."

Mr. Black brought the steaming mugs over to us. His back stiff. No doubt blaming himself for those repercussions that would affect his daughter.

But was it genuine kindness that had brought the principal here to discuss them? Or a manufactured opportunity to plant the murder weapon? Gibson had opportunity, same as Bergström, but once again I was at a loss for a motive.

Mr. Black finished handing out mugs and sat down beside Hallie.

She sent him a look of gratitude before continuing. "The nastier kids have jumped on the news, calling Joy a murderer's daughter and worse." She sought out her husband's hand and gave it a squeeze. "It's all over social media. Gibson knew it was going to happen and wanted to prepare us as best as she could. So you can see what I'm saying, right? She really cares about Joy. More than anyone else in the whole bloody school."

I let Etta make the appropriate responses while my mind turned over the new puzzle piece. If Gibson's care for Joy was part of some devious plan to get away with murder, then she'd been planning this crime for a very long time. Unlikely. But if she really did care for Joy, how could she justify framing Mr. Black?

I thought back to what she'd said about Joy that night at the bar. Something about her being intelligent but a born victim too. My stomach lurched. Surely not?

Mr. Black pushed the battered swear pig over to his wife. And I prayed that I was wrong.

20

HALLIE OFFERED US DINNER, but the sick feeling in my stomach was getting worse. We had to get to the bottom of this. I phoned Mae as soon as we were in the car, explained my theory, and requested she focus her background search on historical events that might support it.

Etta cussed when she understood my reasoning. A subconscious part of me waited for the swear jar to materialize, but of course it didn't.

"What do we do now?" she asked.

"I don't know. I guess we should return this car to Harper's garage while we wait for Mae to dig something up."

She gave her assent, and we drove in silence. It was only as we were transferring the disguises and junk food wrappers to my Corvette that she spoke up again.

"These sunglasses reminded me of something. Do you remember how that nosy neighbor—"

"You mean Mr. Nostril Hairs." I interrupted, trying to lighten the mood.

"Hush, this could be important," she said, but there was a smile in her voice. "Remember how he told us about a woman watching Watts the week before he was killed? He mentioned she was wearing big, buglike sunglasses, similar to these ones. And that she was a brunette in her thirties or forties. Do you think it might've been Gibson?"

I halted for a second, considering. "Good point. Didn't he say she was driving a blue Honda Civic too? I can't believe I didn't think of it when we followed her home. Gibson's car was blue. Well, I think it was blue."

"Yes, hard to be a hundred percent sure in the dark, but I reckon you might be on the mark. There are a lot of Honda Civics in LA though."

"Then why don't we see if the star witness of the case recognizes Gibson from a photo?"

Etta checked the time. "Sure. No one's asleep by nine on New Year's Eve anyway. Mr. Nostril Hairs will probably be glad for the company."

Etta was partially correct.

He was glad to see us, but he'd trimmed his nostril hairs since we'd last visited, so we were going to have to come up with a new nickname.

"I must've died and gone to heaven to have two beautiful angels return to my doorstep on New Year's Eve," he said. "Did you come back to take me up on my offer of a date? I've got a lot of money, and I sure know how to spoil a lady."

He was spoiling the Cheese Puffs and Snickers bar I'd eaten on the way over. It turned out I should've taken Hallie up on her offer of dinner after all.

"Really?" Etta purred. "I might have to experience that for myself, you old player. But first we were wondering if you could help us again. Do you think you'd recognize that lady you saw watching the Watts' home a week and a half ago?"

"Sure I would. I've got a mind like a steel trap. She was loitering on the street, same as you two were on Thursday before those emergency vehicles showed up. I don't know why you didn't come and see me then."

He was referring to the day we'd saved Nicole from the thugs.

"Ah, we were going to," Etta claimed, "but after what happened with Mrs. Watts, we were so traumatized that it fell out of our heads. I guess we don't have such a great memory as you."

"Sure, I can understand that. Not everyone can stay calm and detail oriented in the face of danger," he said modestly.

Etta thrust her phone at him, displaying Gibson's school portrait photo. "Could this be the lady you saw?"

He peered at it, then checked his pockets for his glasses. The longer he searched, the less hope I had of a positive ID. Finally he found them, swinging from his neck on a lanyard-style strap. He put them on the bridge of his nose and peered at the photo again. "Hmm. Yep, it was definitely her. She never got out of the car like you two did, but when Michael drove off, she followed. I didn't see her again after that."

"Not even on the day Mr. Watts was killed?"

"No, I would've told the police if I did. The one stranger I saw was the person they have pegged as the murderer."

It didn't mean much. The shooter could have just as easily accessed the property from the back via the Riviera Country Club. Come to think of it, a set of golf clubs would be the perfect vehicle for carting a gun past security and other curious eyes. And since our murderer had successfully framed Mr. Black, I figured they were good at planning.

"But it's not as if I spend every moment of every day staring out my window," he continued. "I'm a busy man."

"Of course you are," I said. "I guess we better not take up any more of your time."

"Hey now, I've always got time for angels."

Etta smiled. "Well, aren't you sweet. Don't worry, my memory might not be as great as yours, but I won't forget where you live."

We turned tail and fled down the paver stone path to the car.

"Are you sure you weren't an actress?" I asked.

"Course I'm sure."

"Then what were you?" I realized I didn't know. I was positive I must have asked her before, but somehow I'd never gotten a straight answer.

"Oh, all sorts of things. I've lived a long time. But I won't bore you with the details."

She was saved from further prying by Mae calling me back.

"I think I've found what you were looking for," she said. "I have a friend who works in Child Protective Services, and she searched the database for me. Olivia Gibson and Leo Bergström lived in the same foster family for six years. My friend dug up why they were both put into the system too. Gibson's biological parents physically abused her, and Bergström's mother was a junkie, father unknown."

It was the confirmation I'd been looking for, and now it all made a horrible kind of sense.

That just left the teensy-weensy matter of proving it.

Neither Etta, Mae, nor I were in the mood for celebrating New Year's Eve, and Connor was working late. Still trying to catch up on the work he'd put off on my behalf two days ago. I was in bed before the fireworks began.

21

EACH WOMAN HAD BEEN WAXED, tanned, exercised, and starved to perfection. And all I could think as I looked at their bodies was how much I needed a donut.

A donut, shapeless flannel pajamas, and bed. It was too early to be awake, and certainly too early to be surrounded by women in string bikinis. Of course, the string bikinis disappeared during each woman's photo session, and that was worse. The Taste Society had done well in choosing female Shades for the role, as most males would have a difficult time concentrating.

Then again, I was having difficulty staying awake. Connor had woken me ten minutes before midnight and told me he wanted to bring in the new year the right way.

He'd kept me up in a most pleasant fashion, then disappeared for work again before my alarm went off.

To add insult to injury, my hard-won presence here was superfluous. Vanessa wasn't eating until after her shoot. She had a bottle of water she'd brought along but hadn't even cracked the seal on it yet.

It was a terrible start to the new year. Aside from the Connor part.

I supposed I should take an odd sort of pride in Vanessa's unmarred skin, unbloated figure, and healthy digestive system, but that felt too weird, so I went back to listening to the gossip. The hot topic of the morning was thinly veiled gloating. "What a shame that Julie couldn't be here. It's a terrible time for her face to break out."

"Yes and poor Tiff still has that awful rash. I checked in on her before coming here, and her skin looks like she fell on a porcupine."

"Sure, zits or a rash is one thing, but Nadine's husband told me she'd spent all night on the toilet."

And on it went. I zoned out and focused on the star photographer. The one they'd delayed the whole shoot until New Year's Day to work his personal brand of magic.

He was a middle-aged gentleman with a large nose and a ponytail and black leather jacket that were too young for him. From what I could tell, his personality seemed to be that of an oily rag, and I had the growing suspicion that he was so good at taking sensual photographs because he was as lecherous as his nose was long.

"That's right, darling," he drawled, "give me a sexy little pout, show me some desire in those eyes, that's it, gorgeous, now pull your left shoulder back, oh yeah that's good."

I zoned him out too. Stephanie was having her shoot done at the moment. The theme was the Amazon rainforest, so she was posed in front of a green screen with vivid blue butterflies artfully arranged to preserve a modicum of modesty. The butterflies were fake, but there were plenty of living props here, including a sloth, a python, and a jaguar. Their handlers waited with them. Welcome to Hollywood. I was almost looking forward to finding out which woman would be chosen to have the python draped over her naked body.

Vanessa was scheduled next.

"Are you sure you wouldn't like some water?" I asked her as a makeup artist went over the highlights on her face and collarbones one more time.

"I'm fine," she said. The photographer beckoned, and she removed her bikini. "Wish me luck."

As she walked over to the makeshift studio space, Miranda's voice rose over the gossip. "Vanessa and her food adviser sure are close, considering I heard her husband's been bonking the food adviser's brains out."

Vanessa's head jerked back to me. I shook my head frantically, but a blush rose to my cheeks.

"Well they do have an open marriage," one of the other women replied, also louder than necessary.

Vanessa seemed to take my heated cheeks as a sign of guilt rather than innocence. Fury tightened every line of her perfect, naked body.

The oblivious photographer piped up. "All right then. Let me have a look at you." He rubbed his nose as he studied her and then leered. "Hank, we've got a live one. Bring out the jaguar."

I could see Vanessa trying to block it out and focus on the shoot, but even with a jaguar to keep her attention, her eyes kept flicking in my direction.

The photographer snapped a few shots and paused. "You've got this fiery look going that could really work, but you need to soften it a bit so it makes me think you'll be dynamite in the sack rather than wanting to cut off my sack. You got me?"

Unable to watch anymore, I slunk away. Which was how I spotted Miranda slipping Emily a wad of cash. Emily noticed me watching and gave me a familiar smile. The one that told me she despised me and suggested I go screw myself. And suddenly I understood the reason behind her apparent change of heart and friendly conversation about our clients.

I might've protected Vanessa's body from the machinations of the WECS Club, but in liaising with another Shade the way I wasn't supposed to, I'd unwittingly exposed her vulnerability. I was in serious trouble. And suspected I wouldn't be getting that $500 bonus anymore either.

Even worse, if I couldn't outsmart Emily, how was I going to outsmart the real murderer of Michael Watts? The killer who'd led the expert detectives down the precise path of her choosing and was looking like she'd get away with it scot-free.

————

"NO WAY," I TOLD ETTA. "No flippin' way. Are you going senile?"

"Course not. I just want to save Abe from being thrown into prison for a murder he didn't commit more than I want to save my own ass."

Ouch.

"If you've got a better idea, throw it at me, but otherwise I'm doing it. We need evidence, and that's our best shot."

"It's illegal."

"So is gay marriage in a bunch of countries. Doesn't mean it's the wrong thing to do."

Ugh. Etta had an answer to everything. Except how to find evidence incriminating Gibson by legal means.

"What if she comes home and finds you? She'll be able to shoot you and claim it was self-defense."

"Guess I'll have to shoot first then."

I stared at the stubborn old woman, sure she must be made of different stuff than me. But as much as she liked to act like she was invincible, she wasn't. And I was worried about her.

"So are you coming or not?" she asked, oblivious to my train of thought.

"I want the record to show that I absolutely do not condone what you're about to do, and I want no part of it. But I'm coming to stand guard. Not to assist you. I'm there strictly for damage control."

She smirked at me. "Whatever eases your conscience."

I reminded myself that since she thought she was invincible, it probably never occurred to her that I might be doing it to protect her.

"Maybe for damage control you could ask that mechanic friend of yours to temporarily disable Principal Gibson's car. If she can't come home, she can't find me in her house and be upset about it."

I shook my head in disbelief. "So you're just going to go and break into her home in the middle of the day? In broad daylight?"

"I'll wear my harmless-old-lady outfit so no one looks twice. It's the one good thing about gettin' old. It's almost as effective as having an invisibility cloak like in those Harry Potter movies. Besides, there's no such crime as breaking and entering. If I don't damage or steal anything, the worst they can ping me for is trespassing. I'll just pick the lock—"

"Wait, you can pick locks?"

"Of course. Good skill to have. For self-defense, obviously. What if someone locked you up? Anyway, I'll pick the lock and take some photos of the evidence. That should be enough to convince the police to get a warrant—I don't need to tell them where I got the photos. And the warrant will make sure any evidence they find is admissible in the court of law. Then Bob's your uncle. Simple as that."

Somehow I didn't think it would be so simple.

"How do you know all this?" I asked.

She flashed me a smile. "I called Mae, and she gave me tips on the best way to go about it so the evidence is admissible in court and there's minimal risk of going to prison."

Oh boy. I'd had a bad feeling that introducing them could be a mistake. Though to be fair to Mae, Etta would have plunged ahead with this regardless, so it was best she did it with strategy.

"Did she teach you how to pick locks too?" I asked, starting to feel better about Etta's unexplainable skill set.

"Nope. That I knew already. For self-defense, like I said."

Her explanation was thin, but I didn't pry further. It wasn't even close to the top of my list of things to worry about right now.

And while most of me thought Etta was crazy, a small part of me whispered that maybe she was brave and I was a coward.

22

THE DAY OF THE BREAK-IN ARRIVED.

Etta had driven past the Frederick Academy parking lot to confirm that Gibson was still working despite the holidays, and we had Harper to ensure Gibson didn't pop home for a visit. My conversation with Harper had gone something like this:

"You want me to what?" she'd asked.

"To temporarily disable Olivia Gibson's car."

"You know that's illegal, right?"

I'd let out a sigh. "Right."

"Good, so long as we're clear."

The more Etta and I had plotted and planned, the more I felt as if I was involved in some kind of elaborate heist, like in Ocean's Eleven. Except I suspected we were doing a piss-poor job of it.

jSixty agonizingly slow seconds passed. Then another thirty. Even with a quick remembered breath in the middle, I was lightheaded from lack of oxygen by the time the door opened. She moseyed inside as if she had every right to be there.

"Settle down," she crooned. "I can't be worried about you having a stroke when I'm trying to concentrate."

She had a point. No matter how nervous I was, I had to breathe if I was going to be any sort of useful lookout or damage control.

"Nice place," she informed me a few seconds later. "Though she needs a decorator to help liven it up. It has potential but looks a bit too much like a principal's office for my taste. Ooh, except she has a big jar of those licorice stick things. The red ones."

I heard the sound of chewing.

"Etta! You weren't supposed to take anything. Now you can get charged with burglary!"

"Oh hush. I'm eating the evidence so there's nothing to stress about. They won't be able to prove I stole anything without a stool sample, and let me tell you, no policeman's gonna wanna do that."

I choked on the water I'd been in the middle of swallowing.

"She's very tidy and organized. I bet she's one of those people who have a to-do list they actually stick to."

Had she written kill Michael Watts and frame Abraham Black on that list? If so, that would be a useful bit of evidence.

Etta giggled. "You should see her eighties hair and glasses combo in this school photo. Must've been when she first started teaching, but even then she would've been a decade behind the times."

"You're supposed to be looking for evidence. Shouldn't you start on a more likely room? A home office maybe?"

"All right. Don't get your panties in a twist. We have plenty of time. Tell me, are other Australians as chicken-livered as you? I always thought with those dangerous critters you have that it would be a continent full of like-minded people as me. But congratulations on single-handedly putting me off from ever going there."

I suspected she was intentionally irritating me to distract me from my anxiety.

"Well, I thought someone of your years would have the wisdom to be nicer to the person who's helping them on an investigation and supplying them with fresh-baked cookies. I guess we were both wrong. Now have you found an office yet?"

Etta chuckled. "Yeah, you need more of that backbone, dear. You'll go further in life that way." A click of a door sounded. "Ah, this looks more like it. But there sure are a lot of files in here. You know it would go a lot quicker with an extra pair of hands."

"I'm sure that's true, but having an extra pair of hands in prison doesn't make your sentence pass any quicker."

"All right, all right. Where should I start?"

"I don't know. I guess if she has school files, you could look up Jaden and Joy and see if she's got anything in there. But she'd probably keep it separate from official school records, so maybe you should find her personal files."

"So . . . anywhere then?"

"That's why I told you to stop stealing licorice and start looking."

Twenty minutes later, Etta yawned. "I thought breaking into someone's house and looking at their files would be interesting, but it turns out, paperwork's just paperwork, and it's boring no matter what the circumstances."

"I'm glad to hear this won't become a new hobby then."

"I don't know. Being a cat burglar might be more fun. I think I'd look good in a black one-piece, scaling walls and stealing jewels."

I was pretty sure she was kidding. "Remind me what it is you did again, that kept a mind like yours entertained for all those years?"

"This and that, dear. This and that . . . I think I found something."

She fell silent.

"Well, what is it?"

"It's a copy of reports she's filed with Child Protective Services. There are at least a dozen different ones in here."

"Any for Jaden? Or Joy?"

"Yes. Both of them."

"It's a start, but it's not going to be enough to get a warrant. It's a mandatory part of her job after all. It only proves what we already knew—that she suspected Jaden and Joy were being abused."

"You're stating the obvious again," Etta grumbled. "I'll snap some pictures anyway, but I've got over half the files to go."

"It's close to lunchtime. What if Gibson comes home?"

"Your mechanic friend has taken care of that, remember? Stop worrying so much."

"I'd just be concerned about your mental health if you had to wear an unstylish orange jumpsuit day in, day out. Let alone if you were tragically deprived of all your boy toys."

Etta snorted. "I told you, the worst they can get me for is trespassing."

More long minutes passed before she spoke again.

"Aha. This is more like it. There are a few surveillance shots of Michael Watts and the same four addresses Abe was given . . . Yes, this is the box all right. There's more." She let out a low whistle. "Izzy, I don't think this is the first time she's done this. There are a bunch of photos of kids in here, with handwriting on the back. Each one has a date at the top with a list of issues like 'withdrawn, flinches easily, C grade average' and then what seems like progress reports of the kid recovering after she's rescued them from an abusive parent. You need to come and see."

"No. Oh no. Etta, get out now! Gibson just showed up with Bergström. She must've caught a lift."

It was even worse than if she'd come alone. A lot worse.

"YOU NEED TO STALL THEM," Etta told me. "This office is a mess. And I need to get photos of this stuff."

"Stall them? How? We can come back for the photos."

"No way. She has a huge shredder in here. If she notices the house has been disturbed, she might get rid of it. You have to stall them."

I tried to think, but my brain was stuck looping through a litany of cuss words. Then I spied Dudley's leash.

Telling myself I wasn't that memorable, I jumped out of the car, leash in hand, and strode down the street toward Bergström and Gibson. "Fido?" I yelled. Okay, that was a stupid name choice, but I was going to have to roll with it in case they'd heard me. "Where are you, boy?" I made sure my path collided with theirs. "Excuse me, have you seen a dog around here?"

"No, sorry," they said, barely bothering to pause.

"Please. I'm desperate. Could you help me look?"

"Sorry, I'm on my lunch break and need to get back to work. But give me your number. If I see a dog, I'll let you know. What does he look like?"

I had to buy time. "He's the most adorable little thing. White. Fluffy. About six inches tall, maybe seven. And he has the most darling eyes. The color of treacle or maybe more like molasses. And his tongue is as pink as bubble-gum and—"

"Okay, I'll know him when I see him. What was your number?"

Uh-oh. What number should I give her? And how could I make it take enough seconds for Etta to escape? I'd had to rip out the earbuds for my stall tactic to work, and now I had no idea where she was up to.

And she had no idea how badly this was going.

"Um. Let me see." I got my phone out and scrolled through my contacts slowly. "Sorry, now that we don't dial numbers anymore, I can never remember my own. Have to keep it in my contacts." I chuckled.

Gibson twitched with impatience. "Wait. Do I know you from somewhere?"

I kept my head down, over the phone. "Nope, I don't think so."

"Yes, I remember now. Your grandmother. The one that used to be a teacher."

Shit. I might not be memorable, but Etta sure was, even in her harmless-old-lady disguise. I wanted to deny it, but what if Etta came out the front in a minute to let me know she was out of there?

"Oh. That's right. Ha, sorry, I try to block out my more embarrassing memories."

Bergström was now looking at me too intently. "I've seen you around before as well. With your grandmother. You came to my office and demanded I tell the police I sent Abraham Black to beat up Michael Watts."

They exchanged glances.

"Now that I definitely have no recollection of." I smiled, trying to act unconcerned. "Did I do something embarrassing enough to block out?"

Bergström wrapped his hand around my arm. "Why don't you come with us for a minute."

"I can't. I need to find Fido!"

"Fido wasn't white and fluffy as I recall."

"See? Must be the wrong person."

His grip on my arm tightened. "I don't think so. You have a very memorable nervous chuckle."

Damn. So much for the not-being-memorable thing.

I had no choice but to go. My Taser was in my bag and my pepper spray in my pocket, but now that Gibson wasn't looking so friendly, I was pretty sure I was out-manned. Maybe when we caught up with Etta, the odds would be more favorable.

Or maybe Etta was already gone.

"The door's unlocked," Gibson reported. "Not a false alarm then."

Alarm? Crud. She must've had a silent one. No wonder she'd come home with reinforcements.

As soon as we stepped inside, Bergström grabbed me around the waist, pinning both of my arms, and pressed a gun to my head. "Now let's find your companion."

This was bad. This was very, very bad.

Gibson went over to the kitchen counter, near the licorice sticks, and pulled out another gun. Then we walked down a short passage as if they knew exactly where Etta had gone. I was no longer sure whether I wanted her to have left the house or not.

We stopped outside a door that I guessed was the office, and Gibson swung it open.

The room was empty.

My stomach dropped. I was all alone with two bad guys and two guns.

One of the guns prodded my temple. "Tell us where she is."

The window behind the big sturdy desk was open, sheer curtains fluttering in the breeze. Files were scattered over the floor. Even getting taken hostage, I hadn't bought her enough time. "I don't know," I said, hoping my honesty would ring out through my fear.

Gibson headed for the files while my brain registered the three heavy filing cabinets, the cluttered floor-to-ceiling bookshelf on the left wall, and the built-in robe on the right. No wonder Etta had wanted an extra pair of hands. Maybe if I'd been less stubborn or less of a coward, we'd have been gone by the time they showed up.

"They know," Gibson said, holding one of the formal school photos Etta had found. "Do you still make a habit of carrying unregistered weapons? We can make it look like self-defense."

Bergström shifted behind me. "What do they know?" he asked.

She didn't seem to hear him.

"Livvy, I promised you I'd always have your back. Nothing's changed. So talk to me. Tell me what's going on here."

She sighed and gently returned the photo to the floor. "Oh, Leo. I busted my ass my whole damn life to be successful. To not let my past dictate my future. To get away from the brokenness and poverty and abuse we lived in for so long."

"I know. You did good, kid."

A smile flickered around her mouth, then vanished.

"Well, it worked. Or so I thought. Until I started seeing children who were scared to call attention to themselves, who never wanted to take their jackets off even if it was hot, or flinched if you raised your voice." Her voice was thick with emotion. "Children who claimed to be accident-prone but never boasted about how they broke their arm. And it was like I was right back there. I realized money doesn't solve the brokenness or the abuse. It just makes it easier to cover up."

She swiped angrily at a stray tear. "I couldn't let those kids live through that. I tried the official channels, but it almost never went anywhere . . ."

"I know how it goes," Bergström agreed.

"Then one of the abusive bastards died in a car accident, and it gave me an idea." She seemed to stand straighter. "Six months later, I orchestrated an accident for another sicko. The kids transformed, Leo. You should've seen how they came out of their shells."

Bergström was silent for a minute, processing the news that his friend was a murderer. A vigilante serial killer to be exact.

"Wow." He said the word softly. "Why didn't you ever tell me all those years?"

She looked solemnly past my right shoulder. Into my captor's eyes, I assumed. "Because I know how much it meant to you that I got out. That I was happy and successful . . . But I shouldn't have involved one of your men—shouldn't have asked you to have Black beat up Watts—without letting you in on the plan. I'm sorry. It just seemed like the perfect opportunity to take out two bastards with one stone."

The grip on my arms had loosened, and I debated stomping down on his foot as hard as I could and ripping free the way Connor had shown me once, but it was still two guns against a Taser, which would take me too long to dig out of my bag.

"You sure about Black?" Bergström asked. "He's always struck me as soft, and he seems to love his girl."

"He does!" I interjected. "She does parkour, this military obstacle course thingy which is how she keeps hurting herself."

The grip tightened again, and I cursed myself for reminding them I was there.

"Even if that's true, it's too late now," Gibson said, ignoring me and addressing Bergström. "Those kids need me, and I'm not going to jail for this. So do you have any unregistered weapons or what?"

He hesitated, just long enough for me to start hoping. Then he said, "Yes, I have one in the car."

My hope squashed like a slug under a shoe.

"Good. We'll deal with her and then go find her grandma. She could barely walk, so she can't have gotten far."

I supposed the harmless-old-lady outfit was paying

unexpected dividends. For Etta. Not so much for the one of us who hadn't wanted to be here in the first place.

Bergström released me.

Since he'd first taken me captive, all I'd wanted to do was get away, but I wasn't stupid. He'd only let go so he didn't shoot at point-blank range. Difficult to claim self-defense then.

It would be difficult to claim self-defense if he shot me in the back too, but he was between me and the door, and Gibson was between me and the window. I couldn't keep my back to both of them. But maybe I could get my Taser somehow . . .

I was still frozen in indecision when Bergström spun me around and gave me a hard shove. I stumbled backward into the bookshelf, and he raised his gun.

"Nooo!"

Out of the corner of my terrified eye, I saw a white shape hurtle toward Bergström.

Bergström pivoted and pulled the trigger.

Blood blossomed in a rapidly expanding circle on my would-be rescuer's giant chest. His white shirt the perfect, horrific showcase.

But it was like trying to stop the momentum of a freight train with a peanut. Mr. Black crashed into Bergström, and they both plummeted to the floor. Bergström's head bounced on the carpet, then neither of them moved.

My ringing ears registered another gunshot, but my eyes were glued to the unmoving Hulk. The man I'd held a grudge against. The man who had a wife and daughter he loved more than anything. The man who'd just taken a bullet for me.

23

I CRAWLED OVER TO HIM, an abstract part of me noticing that I was sobbing hysterically, snot dripping down my chin. Like his blood, oozing onto the carpet.

Fingers touched his neck. "He's alive, Izzy. It's okay, he's alive." Etta's head swam into my vision. She swiped away the hair that was sticking to the wetness on my face. "Come on. The ambulance is on its way. Help me roll him over so we can slow the bleeding."

I'm sure that in any other circumstances, rolling Mr. Black would've been impossible. But as Etta's words brought hope to my heart, we found the strength.

It helped that he had the inert body of Bergström beneath him to use as a kind of fulcrum to pivot on.

Etta's hands guided mine to the center of the sticky crimson patch on his chest. "Press here. Hard. Imagine it's your ex-husband's head in a bathtub. I'll make sure Gibson and Bergström are properly disarmed."

It could've been seconds or hours later when men in blue uniforms shifted my hands and miraculously maneuvered Mr. Black onto a gurney. Lucky it was one of those modern hydraulic ones that raised itself off the ground, or that might have been as far as they got.

"Will he be okay?" I croaked.

"We'll do everything we can," they said. The same promise I'd made to Joy when I didn't have any hope to offer her. The promise I'd made about saving her dad.

As they wheeled him out of my sight, I noticed that two more teams were dealing with Bergström and Gibson. Gibson was bleeding too. Had Etta shot her?

"Well," Etta said under her breath. "That was some stalling you did. Now we better get our stories straight before we're questioned . . ."

The police officers who'd responded to the 911 call kindly allowed me to wash the snot from my face and the blood from my hands. If only I could wash away my guilt so easily. I couldn't understand how what had started out as me begrudgingly helping Mr. Black clear his name had ended with him taking a bullet for me. Even prison was better than a coffin. Every fiber of me was strung tight, desperately hoping he'd be okay. The thought of explaining his last act of heroism to Joy and Hallie made me want to crumple to the floor. The floor stained with his blood.

The officer was asking me questions, and I was trying to stick to Etta's improvised version of events, but I couldn't concentrate. Truthfully, I wasn't sure how Etta had come to be hiding in the built-in robe, able to spring out at the moment of Mr. Black's distraction to take out Gibson. And I didn't have the faintest idea about how Mr. Black had known I was in trouble and come to my rescue.

We must have been at the scene for at least an hour before one of the officers suggested we go down to the station to answer some more questions. Numbly I obeyed, despite a twinge in the back of my mind that there was something wrong with that plan. Etta took one look at my face and asked for the car keys.

"You better ring Connor," she said. "You don't look so good."

"I'm okay. I'm just afraid for Mr. Black."

"Don't be. He'll be fine." Her words were cheerful, but I could hear the underlying worry. "It would take more than a single tiny bullet to take down such a strong man. Plus we got immediate pressure to the wound and zipped him off to the hospital real quick. You'll see."

Her phone dinged to let her know she had a message,

and she read it while driving. I didn't have it in me to tell her off for it.

"Ha. Told you so. Hallie says the bullet missed anything vital, and he's out of surgery already. The doc's expecting he'll make a full recovery."

Relief didn't flood me, but it trickled into my system and slowly spread, returning life to my numb limbs.

I called Connor. Mostly because if I didn't, it would set a very low bar for the new standard of communication I was trying to establish in our relationship.

"Good news and bad news," I told him. "The good news is, we found out who killed Michael Watts, and the police now have evidence to that effect."

"And the bad news?"

"Well, I kind of got taken hostage, and they were going to shoot me and then arrange things so it looked like self-defense, but then Mr. Black and Etta came to my rescue except Mr. Black got shot in the process, but the doctor said he's going to be okay, so I guess that's kind of good news too." I said it all in one breath, like if I got it out fast enough he might miss it.

"Hostage?" His tone was a tad scary.

Guess he didn't miss it.

"Kind of taken hostage," I reiterated. "And I didn't get shot or anything."

"Where are you?"

"On our way to the police station to answer more questions. Maybe you could get a transcript so I don't have to go through it all a third time."

"Isn't Hunt leading this investigation?"

Crap. That was the thing my mind had tried to warn me about. "Um."

"Did you do anything that might be construed as illegal? Because he has it out for you and he's not going to be pleased about you showing him up on another case."

I hadn't done anything illegal, had I? Except, did watching Etta break in make me complicit? Oh yeah, and getting Harper to disable Gibson's car. A fat lot of good that had done.

Connor exhaled in resignation when I didn't respond. "I'll come down to the station and see what I can do."

"No. If Hunt realizes you have a vested interest in me, he'll realize you had an ulterior motive for finding the drugs in Watts's car, and then he'll make any future cases you work on together hell. Besides, he might go easier on me if we don't piss him off with that revelation. And even if I skirted the edge of a law here or there, he has no proof. It'll be Etta's and my word against a serial killer's and her sidekick's."

His voice grew low and quiet. The way it did when he was really mad. "Did you just say serial killer?"

"Um. Only of bad guys. Anyway, I better go so Etta and

I have a chance to work on the details of our story, but I'm okay, and I'll see you later."

"If you're not out of that police station in three hours, I'm coming in whether you like it or not."

"Got it. And um, thanks."

I disconnected and sent Harper a text telling her to fix Gibson's car and wipe off any prints. Then I deleted the message.

There, now Hunt couldn't find any hard evidence against me.

Despite my bravado with Connor, the idea of being interrogated by Hunt made my cheeks clench. All four of them. By the time Etta parked outside the station, I'd worked myself into a cold sweat. I was emotionally wrung out. If Hunt decided to toss my ass in jail for another night, it would break me. And I needed to see that Mr. Black would be okay with my own eyes, or I wouldn't be able to sleep without nightmares. Maybe not even then.

The dreary front of the 27th Street Community Police Station did nothing to allay my fears. I followed Etta inside like a condemned woman walking to her lethal injection. I hadn't even gotten a last meal of my choosing.

All too soon, Hunt was looming in front of me, his eyes like blue chips of ice. "We'll interview them separately," he said to the officer standing at his side. "You take her, I'll take this one."

I started after him until a hand tapped my shoulder. "Excuse me, Miss, we'll talk in here."

The hand belonged to an African-American woman with a kind smile. I looked back at Hunt who was guiding Etta to an interrogation room. Etta's step was light and airy as if they were on their way to collect fairy floss. I felt a stab of dismay for her, then steeled myself to hold up my end of the story.

Officer Green probably asked me the same kind of questions Hunt would have, but she asked them in a warm, understanding way that made it an entirely different experience. It was still tiring and designed to detect any lies on my part, but she made me feel safe. Almost. Unfortunately, that meant that when I explained again how Mr. Black had been shot trying to save me, her sympathy peeled away my fragile facade, and I bawled my eyes out. She passed me some tissues, brought me another cup of tea, asked a few last questions, and offered me a ride home.

"Thanks, but I'll wait for my friend," I said.

The thought of how Etta might be faring with Hunt made me want to cry some more. She was tough of course, but Hunt was tougher, and I felt guilty that I'd gotten off so lightly. It didn't help that she had actually broken the law. What if Hunt trapped her into admitting it? She was smart, but then she wasn't nearly scared enough of prison as she should be. If he set her up the right way, she might even boast about it.

She came out about twenty minutes later, the same spring to her step she'd walked in there with. If her little-old-lady outfit had taught me anything, though, it was that she was a superb actress.

I went to her and looped my arm through hers, waiting until we'd left the building (a feat that in itself made me feel about a hundred times better) to ask, "How did it go with Hunt? Are you okay?"

"Yes, it was fine. He invited me to dinner actually."

My arm tightened around hers, pulling us to a stop. "What?" Maybe I'd lost it. Maybe I was hearing things. "Did you say yes?"

She looked at me, her face neutral. "I might have."

When I didn't say anything else, she tugged impatiently. "Come on, don't you want to see Abe?"

"But"—I searched around for a reason that didn't give away Taste Society secrets and Hunt and my history together—"didn't you tell me he was too old for you?"

Too old meaning a mere five odd years younger than her.

She lifted her chin. "Well yes, but I thought it best to keep him on my good side. Since our story about how we ended up in that shoot-out is a touch thin. Now come on, let's go."

I allowed her to pull me along. I was incapable of stringing together a single coherent sentence anyway.

We reached the parking lot, and there, leaning against my Corvette, was the best thing I'd seen all day.

Connor put the thermos and bakery bag down on the roof of the car and wrapped me in a long, hard hug. We stood like that for a while. His body telling me more clearly than words ever could of how relieved he was to know that I was safe and whole. And as I returned his embrace with Etta looking on and giving me a thumbs up, it occurred to me that perhaps it wasn't such a bad start to the new year after all.

———

MR. BLACK SEEMED TO BE FALLING out of both sides of the hospital bed at once. His tan skin was several shades lighter than normal, and instead of the usual white dress shirt that I always thought must've been specially altered to fit around his biceps, he was wearing a typical hospital gown that he somehow managed to make a snug fit.

His gentle brown eyes lit up when Etta, Connor, and I entered.

"How are you feeling?" I asked.

"Never better," he lied.

I licked my lips. "Thank you. For saving my life."

"I could say the same thing to you. If I'd had to go to prison and leave my girls behind, I wouldn't have had a life worth living, but a nice policeman came in an hour ago and told me they're dropping all charges." His smiled so broadly I could count his molars.

Etta clapped her hands. "That's fabulous news, Abe. We always knew you were innocent."

Well, one of us had.

He was still beaming. "Thank you for believing in me when no one else would. Especially you, Ms. Avery, after what I did."

My honesty wanted me to admit that I hadn't, not at first, but a confession would only clear my conscience and sadden his. "How did you manage to come to my rescue at that critical moment?" I asked instead.

"Well. Ever since I got fired and then Etta told me about that firebomb in your apartment, I was worried about you. I didn't want you to get hurt for my sake. So I started following you, from a distance so I didn't get in your way, but close enough that I could help if anything went wrong."

He'd been protecting us for days, and we'd never even spotted him. Great detectives we were.

It confirmed my suspicions that if Mae ever did surveillance on me, I'd never know.

"It's lucky you did," Etta said. "I was hiding in the cupboard waiting for a chance to take them down, but I couldn't figure out how to do it without risking Izzy. Darned if I know how I would've rescued her ass without you."

I coughed. Yeah sure, she'd rescued me. I would never have been in that mess if it wasn't for her.

Connor's lip twitched with amusement.

Hallie and Joy saved the situation by returning from the canteen. There was much hugging and thanking and watery eyes all round. Except for Connor who'd planted himself in the corner with his back to a wall as if the rest of us were volatile entities.

I guess to be fair, compared to Mr. Ocean of Calm Composure we were volatile. That and the last kid he'd seen had vomited on his shoes.

"Ms. Avery?" Joy asked. "Can I talk to you for a minute?"

"Sure."

We stepped out into the hospital hallway. "I wanted to thank you again. I know you took the case on mostly for Mum and me, and Etta said how your house got burned down in the process. I'm sorry about that."

"It's okay," I told her. "It was only stuff that burned. Stuff can be replaced, not like people. And you're welcome."

She threw her spindly arms around me again, and I thought again about how smart she was. Mature, as well as smart. Then as she stepped back, I noticed the Disney Princess watch strapped to her wrist. The one I'd used as a bargaining chip with Mr. Black the day he'd come to terrify me into paying my debt. "Can I ask you something?"

She nodded. "Of course."

"That watch of yours, um, does it have some special meaning?"

She glanced down at it. "You mean why am I wearing a commercialized fairy-tale product that promotes the idea that women need to be rescued?"

"Uh, yes." Never mind that I'd needed rescuing by her father hours earlier.

She spun it around her wrist, the band way too big for her even on its smallest adjustment. "Dad bought it for me a couple of years ago, and he was so sure I'd love it, I didn't have the heart to tell him otherwise."

I grinned. "You two are lucky to have each other."

We returned to the crowded hospital room where Hallie was giving Etta a rundown on the incredibly fortunate trajectory the bullet had taken through Mr. Black's torso.

When she'd finished, I heard myself asking him, "How did you get that scar on your cheek?"

It was an inch-long jagged scar on his left side that lent a menacing edge to his visage and had helped scare the pants off me when we'd first met.

"Oh, Joy's kitten got stuck up a tree a few years ago. I climbed up a ladder to help the poor thing down, but the ladder slipped and a branch caught my face as I fell." He smiled, the scar creasing his cheek. "The kitten was fine if you were wondering."

Man, almost all my preconceived ideas about Mr. Black had proven false. My mum had taught me over and over to make an effort to understand things from the other person's perspective, but I hadn't thought it applied to the bruiser who'd come to beat me up on behalf of my loan shark. Guess I should've known better. She would love to hear me admit she was right. As always.

"So how long until you're outta here?" Etta asked him.

"The doctor said I could go home in about five more days and that it'll be another week after that until I'm back to my old self. Except I won't be allowed to do any heavy lifting for a while."

I wondered how they'd pay the bills in the meantime without Mr. Black—Abe—having a job. He might have been thinking along the same lines, because he ran a giant paw over his giant head as he was apt to do and admitted, "I was kind of relieved to be fired from that job. But I hope I can find something else soon."

Etta patted his hand. "You'll find something. But I wouldn't ask Mr. Bergström for a reference. You flattened him like a pancake."

I glanced over at Connor, who was still standing in the corner, and an idea popped into my head. "How do you feel about protecting people or places for a living? I know someone who works in security."

"I think I'd enjoy that," he said.

"Great. I'll give them a call and see if they've got anything available."

We stayed and made small talk for a few more minutes until a nurse came and kicked us out. Apparently, there was supposed to be a limit of two visitors at a time.

As Connor and I strolled down the hospital corridor, he wrapped an arm around my waist. "So you know someone who works in security, do you?"

I was relieved to hear a faint hint of amusement in his voice.

"Not just someone. A very special someone." I batted my lashes at him. "Do you think you could you give him a job?"

"I need people I can trust. Do you trust him?"

I thought about him carrying Dudley up and down the stairs for Etta, the tears in his eyes when Joy and Hallie rushed to see him after his bail hearing, the scar on his face from saving a darn kitten, and the panicked shout of "no" as he ran at the man who'd been about to shoot me. "Yes. I trust him," I said, surprising myself with the answer.

Connor nodded once. "Okay. I'll offer him a position with a probationary period. It will be useful if he works out. I'm short-staffed at the moment with a couple of my guys on paternity leave. It's the main reason I've been so busy the last few days."

I couldn't believe it had been less than seventy-two hours since we'd taken down Scrawny Scientist together. Or that Connor had just volunteered some information about his company. But the biggest revelation was that he trusted me enough to take a chance on a bruiser he didn't know from Adam.

I hoped he wouldn't regret it. I wanted him to one day trust me enough to take a chance on sharing his deepest self too.

"Um, there's one thing you should know first," I said.

His lips flattened. "What?"

"Mr. Black gets nauseous at the sight of blood."

Connor stopped and stared at me, wondering if I was joking. Then he resumed walking. "Remind me never to hire you in a recruiting role."

"On the bright side, a person only bleeds after you hurt them, right? So he should only faint or throw up after he takes down the bad guys."

24

A WEEK LATER, I picked Oliver up from the airport like the nice housemate I am, figuring I needed all the brownie points I could get after burning down the apartment. With a lot of help from Mae, Etta, and Connor, I'd finally finished fixing it up last night, but I was nervous about how Oliver would react to the radical makeover. So for an extra measure of goodwill, I brought Meow with me. She was one of those rare cats that didn't mind car travel.

I let her out of the carrier, and she launched herself at him as soon as he slipped inside. His answering grin had tears pricking my eyes. A minute after pulling out of the pickup lane, Oliver was stretched back in his seat, with Meow purring on his chest, her one black paw resting on his collarbone the way it did when she wanted further attention.

"It's good to be home," Oliver said, contentment oozing from him like slime from a car salesman. He slid a look toward me. "That is, if I have a home to come back to."

"Well, there's much more IKEA than there used to be, but I hope it'll still feel like home."

Connor and I had spent all of yesterday constructing IKEA furniture. You can learn a lot about a person doing that. I'd learned that, for someone who could afford fully assembled furniture, he was irritatingly competent at putting it together. He'd finished assembling two chairs by the time I'd done one, and after that, he kept finding excuses to get me out of the way like you would a child:

"I'd love a cup of tea." Hint, hint, nudge, nudge.

"Maybe you should sit on the couch"—that he'd constructed—"and make sure it's comfortable enough."

"You must be starving. Did you want to organize lunch?"

Meow had conspired with him by deciding that screws were almost as much fun to play with as cockroaches, and keeping track of her new toys had become a full-time job until I'd shut her in my bedroom.

My irritation at his competence had lessened after I'd snuck some TV cabinet drawers into my bedroom after Meow and painstakingly assembled them. I could do it, but it wasn't as fun as it looked. And when I'd returned from a quick trip to the grocery store to restock the fridge, and Connor told me to go see what Meow had done to my bed, my irritation faded entirely.

Gone was the horrible rainbow-vomit duvet cover. He'd replaced it with a simple navy one. In all the furniture selection for the rest of the house, I'd completely forgotten about my resolution.

I wandered out to where Connor was sitting on one of the new armchairs, Meow on his lap.

"How did you know I hated that thing?"

"I didn't. I only knew I hated it," he said. "But I figured even your fashion sense couldn't be bad enough to like it."

I threw myself down beside him, making sure a stray elbow clocked him in the ribs, then leaned my head on his shoulder. "Just remember, you're the one that fell for me."

He slipped an arm around me. "And so far, I don't even regret it."

I stopped at a traffic light and pulled myself back to the present. Oliver was having his own romantic moment with Meow, so he hadn't noticed my lapse. "How was your trip?" I asked him.

"Let's just say it reminded me of all the reasons why I live in LA. The weather was horrid. The Queen was constantly on TV. And my family was, well, my family. Here, I snapped a picture for you."

It was a photo of Oliver standing among his family. I could tell they were family because they all had the same curly blond hair and similar facial features. But while they were wearing conservative dress shirts and pants, Oliver was sporting a black T-shirt that announced in bold white letters: "I pooped today!"

A stick figure holding a roll of toilet paper high in victory illustrated the concept.

"So you're kind of the odd one out, huh?" I said.

"I prefer to consider it as being the one independent thinker of the bunch. I'm not a sheep needing to follow after the herd. It's the same reason I haven't been brainwashed into worshipping Her Royal Majesty."

"Considering your choice of T-shirts, Her Royal Majesty might be pleased about that."

He snorted. "You know I always aim to please. Now tell me what's been happening around here."

I told him, much to his amusement. But as I followed him up the stairs to our renovated apartment, I was apprehensive about how he'd react.

He opened the door, took half a dozen steps inside, and fell to his knees. "The beautiful wallpaper. It's gone! I knew the furniture was a write-off, but you didn't tell me about the wallpaper. Do you know how many hours it took me to draw eyes on all those pineapples? And how many girls I brought home that were creeped out by those eyes? And the new table is nice enough, but what about my Ninja Turtle stickers? Even that filthy green carpet held so many memories. Like the stain from when you tried to make squid ink pasta and Meow got into it then vomited it back up."

Meow wriggled out of his arms as if in protest at the memory.

I looked around. It was a vast improvement. The walls and ceiling were freshly painted white, and the musty green carpet had been replaced with a sensible blue-and-gray fleck. Regrettably, the half-a-century-old linoleum had been deemed okay. That stuff was invincible. I'd chosen muted blue couches and a simple white TV cabinet, coffee table, and dining set. Plus I'd lashed out on a thirty-inch flat screen, a few throw cushions, and a houseplant. The effect was far from glamorous, but it was serviceable and had a calming, fuss-free vibe.

Except for the houseplant, which I was almost certain to kill.

I went over to Oliver, who was still kneeling on the new carpet. "I thought you might feel that way, so I got you some housewarming gifts. I know it's not housewarming in a traditional sense, but maybe it'll help you warm to the house." I gave him the two presents I'd wrapped.

He tore them open, and a smile crept across his face. "I love them. Thank you." He walked over to the table and stuck down the new Ninja Turtle stickers, then looked at the remaining gift.

"I actually took the liberty of putting a hook up for you," I pointed out.

In the middle of the bright white wall that had once featured the hideous wallpaper was a hook. He hung the frame up on it. It was a piece of the old wallpaper, complete with creepy pineapple eyes. He stepped back and admired it before turning to me. "You're officially forgiven."

———

WITH MR. BLACK CLEARED of all charges, the apartment fixed, Oliver back, and Mae planning to return to her home in San Bernardino County tomorrow, we decided to hold our own belated New Year's party.

Connor had kindly offered to host. Probably thanks to some heavy-handed hints on Mae's part.

Moments before Oliver, Etta, Dudley, Meow, and I were due to leave, a UPS guy delivered a large parcel. There was a note attached.

Isobel,
Turns out the angry, sultry look really works on me. I was René Laurent's top pick for the Scandalous Cause calendar. I also realized you're nothing like my husband's type. He

tends to appreciate the finer things in life.
Take care, Vanessa

Inside the box was a great deal of bubble wrap and tissue paper, and underneath all that, a vase. At least I thought it was a vase. It was the color of our old carpet, overlaid with ornate white-robed figures and what looked like a goat.

It was hideous.

I had no idea whether Vanessa meant it as a genuine gift, was getting rid of an unwanted Christmas present, or whether the ugliness of the piece was a reflection of her feelings toward me.

Oliver wandered out of the bedroom, Meow clinging to him as if he might abandon her again.

"Holy cow, Iz. That looks like a Wedgewood."

"A wedge what?"

"A Wedgewood. It's a famous old pottery brand. Even older than the Queen. And if that's a genuine piece, it'd be worth at least two grand. Maybe three."

I stared at him, unsure whether my incredulity was due more to its estimated value or the idea that Oliver would admit to recognizing something so pretentiously materialistic.

"What?" His tone was defensive. "My mother loves them. But then she loves the Queen too, so I guess I shouldn't be surprised."

He came over and picked it up.

"Careful," I said, suddenly feeling protective of the ugly thing. A couple grand would go a long way toward covering some of the furniture I'd had to buy.

He tipped it upside down and looked at the bottom of it. "Yep, it's got the Wedgewood mark on it, see?" He put it down and grabbed the note. "Who's Vanessa?"

Damn. I could hardly pass that off as a nickname for Connor.

"Someone I did a favor for."

He whistled. "Must've been some favor."

"It was," I lied. Then I carried it into my bedroom, laid it down on my new duvet cover, and promised that I'd list it on eBay tomorrow.

Connor and Harper were making cocktails when we arrived. His hands were full, and he wasn't prone to public displays of affection, but his eyes lit up when he saw me, and that was better than if he'd run over and twirled me around in his arms.

The Tudor mansion included an entertainment room complete with its own kitchenette-cum-bar. How handy. Mae was sitting on a couch with her feet up, a half-empty dirty martini in hand, and a glittery pink party hat on her head.

"It's time we share our New Year resolutions," she announced. "Who wants to start?"

No one volunteered.

"All right, I will then. This year I'm going to try to win a prize at the San Bernardino County Distillery Club for my gin, and I'm going to come back to LA for a few extra visits. Since my children could obviously benefit from some more maternal guidance."

Connor and Harper exchanged glances. Etta and I snickered. Oliver raised the glass he'd just been given and said, "Mine's kind of the opposite of yours. I will again resolve not to aspire to any levels of fame, and I'll return to England as rarely as possible because my family doesn't appreciate my guidance anyway." Then, bartender that he was, he wandered over to study the liquor collection.

That at least made me feel better about my own lack of resolution. I didn't want to admit to the duvet cover thing.

Seeing Oliver and Harper in close proximity had me hoping they might hook up. They were both laid-back, playful souls who could be wonderful for each other. But Oliver only had eyes for the alcohol and Harper was thinking hard, trying to come up with her own resolution.

"I've got one," she said. "I'm going to convince Connor to purchase a car that isn't black." She punched him in the arm. "What about you, brother?"

He grunted and kept making cocktails.

"If you won't participate, we'll have to come up with one for you," Mae threatened.

"I'll go first!" Harper sang a little too quickly. "This year Connor will try to be less . . . well . . . Connor-ish."

I smirked. "And he'll start talking so much that one of us will actually need to tell him to shut up."

We all snickered some more.

Etta sipped her drink, then held up her hand. "My turn. He'll invite Izzy to move in with him . . . permanently." Everyone oohed. "And then invite me and Dudley too," she added, "since there's plenty of room."

Dudley was stretched out on one of Connor's designer couches looking very content with himself. I figured that meant he was amenable to the idea.

When we finished laughing, I pointed a finger at Etta. "What about you? I hope your New Year resolution includes no more amateur sleuthing in the coming twelve months."

She put down her drink with a thud. "Are you kidding me? We saved an innocent man from going to jail, kept a loving family together, rescued a grieving widow and her son, and took down a frigging serial killer! I'm just getting started!"

Everyone laughed.

Except me.

Or Connor, naturally.

Then I noticed Mae wasn't laughing either. "Actually, she's not kidding. We've been talking about it, and we're going to revive my old PI firm and go into business together."

Silence reigned. Harper had frozen with her drink half-way to her mouth. Connor had the clearest emotion I'd ever seen on his face. It was horror.

Then Etta sniggered, and she and Mae collapsed into merry hysterics, clutching their stomachs like they might burst.

Despite the realization that I'd been pranked—again—the sound of their mirth failed to completely wash away my unease.

FROM THE AUTHOR

I hope you loved POISON IS THE NEW BLACK. That way I can rub it in my brother's smug face since he scoffed at me when I first started writing at the tender age of sixteen. If you want to help me make sure he gets his comeuppance, take a minute to leave me a review or mention this book to a friend who'll also enjoy it. That'll show him.

As a small token of my appreciation for everyone who already did this for other books in the series, I drew you this picture of my brother sulking on the floor. Enjoy!

My brother sulking on the floor

ACKNOWLEDGEMENTS

A huge thank you to my readers for giving me an excuse to spend all day, every day with the people in my head instead of having to venture into the real world.

Sincere gratitude to my incredible beta readers, Tess, John, Rosie, Bec, James, and Mum, who have not only read every book twice but are also very forgiving of my lack of social skills. I'm not quite as bad as a club-dragging Neanderthal, but still.

To the proofreaders and final pass editors at Victory Editing, thank you again for pointing out my every mistake. You guys should meet my older brother sometime. I think you'd get along.

To my husband, thank you for being nothing like my big brother. That doesn't mean I'm going to let you keep that beard though.

And to God, for His grace and patience in loving me through every hurdle that comes my way—whether real or invented by my own imagination (SPOILER: It's mostly the latter).

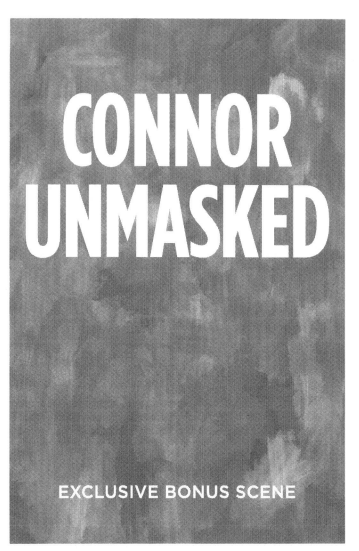

CONNOR UNMASKED

EXCLUSIVE BONUS SCENE

Want to know what Connor thought of Izzy when they first met?

Read this BONUS scene in his perspective & find out!

For a full list of books by the author, please visit:
CHELSEAFIELDAUTHOR.COM

82701934R00190

Made in the USA
Columbia, SC
05 December 2017